THE DUMMY

The Dummy

& Other Uncanny Stories

by

Nicholas Royle

Swan River Press
Dublin, Ireland
MMXXII

The Dummy
by Nicholas Royle

Published by
Swan River Press
Dublin, Ireland
December MMXXII

www.swanriverpress.ie
brian@swanriverpress.ie

Cover design by Meggan Kehrli
from artwork © Bill Bulloch

Set in Garamond by Ken Mackenzie

Paperback Edition
ISBN 978-1-78380-765-9

Swan River Press published
a limited hardback edition of
The Dummy in July 2018.

Contents

The Other Man

Every morning the same routine. Graeme's wife would stir first and he would wake while she was getting out of bed to go to the bathroom. While she was performing her ablutions, he would lever himself into a sitting position and swivel around, slipping his feet into a pair of Chinese slippers. Slowly, with effort that seemed to increase week by week, he would stand up and walk to the bedroom door, where he would take his dressing gown from the hook and put it on. He would climb the stairs to the second floor, the ease or difficulty with which he performed this act tending to depend on the time he had gone to bed the night before. He would clean his teeth and use the toilet and then walk back down to the first floor, where the light from under the bathroom door would indicate that his wife was still within, and he would continue downstairs, where he would switch the alarm off and go into the kitchen and make them both a cup of tea. He would take the tea upstairs and usually by this stage his wife would be out of the bathroom and he would hand one of the cups to her and she would say thank you as she took it from him and started to get dressed.

One particular day, while his wife—Sarah—was in the bathroom, he arranged his pillow and one of Sarah's pillows and a couple of cushions under the duvet on his side of the bed and crept up the stairs to the second floor. But he got his timing wrong and came back down just as Sarah was emerging from the bathroom, so he snuck back into the bedroom and remade the bed.

The next day, he arranged the pillows and cushions under the duvet again and went up to the top floor, taking care lest the stairs should creak. When Graeme came back down, Sarah had finished in the bathroom and he could hear her voice in the bedroom. He peeped through the crack of the door. She was sitting on the edge of the bed towelling the ends of her hair. She had stopped speaking for a moment, as if waiting for a response from beneath the duvet.

With care, he retreated from the door and walked downstairs. He quickly disarmed the alarm and then shut the kitchen door behind him so that she would not hear him boiling the kettle. He stood and looked out of the window while waiting. The same damp lawn, bare trees, grey sky as the day before and the day before that. The kettle clicked off.

He climbed the stairs quietly and paused outside the bedroom door, hearing voices. It did sound like there was more than one.

There was a bookcase on the landing. Graeme deposited the cups of tea on top of it and placed his eye at the crack of the door. He couldn't see Sarah, who had perhaps moved to the right of the doorway. She would be leaning over the chest of drawers where she kept her make-up and jewellery, studying her face in the mirror. But on his side of the bed, the duvet had been pulled back and a shape like a pillow standing on its end appeared to have been somehow propped up on the edge of the mattress. The shape moved forwards slightly and then started to twist around to one side and something caught in Graeme's throat.

He backed away from the door. What his brain told him his eyes had seen he couldn't have. A mask, perched on top of the pillow: line and shade, the suggestion of a face.

He moved back to the door. Sarah's voice could be heard from inside the bedroom.

"Right, well, some of us have got to go to work."

He registered the business-like jangle of her charm bracelet.

The shape that had been sitting on his side of the bed stood up and stretched rudimentary arms, its back to the room. It was the size—and more or less the shape—of a man. It turned around and Graeme heard a voice that wasn't Sarah's.

"Have a nice day, darling."

It was what he would normally say, but to him the words sounded badly pitched. There was a mouth-like slit in the mask, which even as Graeme watched was resolving into something more like a human face. Could Sarah not see, though, that the figure standing before her was not him, was not Graeme, was not even actually human? Its movements were all wrong, its dimensions slightly off. But only slightly. And as he watched, the amount by which they were off seemed to get smaller, and the movements became more natural. The eyes looked less like buttons. As the figure walked around the end of the bed, Graeme had to concede it was like looking in the mirror. The figure passed out of view and Graeme heard Sarah's bracelet jingle. He imagined them embracing; he heard them kiss. Then he made out the rustle of Sarah turning to move towards the door and he backed off and ran, as carefully as he could, up the stairs to the next floor.

He watched through the spindles as his wife and this other man walked out of the bedroom together. The man was dressed, in *his* clothes.

"See you later," Sarah shouted as she reached the ground floor.

"See you later," Graeme muttered quietly at the same time as he heard the other man say the same words, more loudly, loudly enough to be heard by Sarah as she opened the front door and left the house.

Graeme remained crouched by the banisters at the top of the house.

Nothing happened. The other man had gone downstairs and Graeme couldn't hear anything. He crept back down to the first floor and slipped into the bedroom. He dressed quickly, moving with more confidence. He went downstairs; he didn't walk on tiptoes, but nor did he proceed in quite the normal way. Stopping at the bottom of the stairs, he listened. The other man was in the kitchen. Graeme could hear him emptying breakfast cereal into a bowl, returning the box to the cupboard, getting the milk from the fridge and a spoon from the drawer. Graeme heard a chair being pulled back as the other man sat down at the table. Graeme listened to the sound of him eating. He remembered his sister once telling him about the noise he made eating corn flakes. He had taken offence, but had henceforth made more of an effort with his table manners. From what Graeme could hear, the other man was eating nicely with his mouth closed. From time to time, his spoon dinked against the side of the bowl. There was a final clarion of cutlery against pottery and what might have been a faint slurp before Graeme heard the chair legs scrape backwards on the wooden floor. He ducked sideways across the hall into the front room as he heard the bowl being lodged in the dishwasher and the other man's footsteps approaching the kitchen door. Graeme held his breath, but the next sound he heard was the creak of the stairs. When the other man would have reached the top of the stairs, or at least gone beyond the half-landing, Graeme stepped back into the hall and then into the kitchen. He opened the dishwasher; there was the other man's dirty bowl on the top shelf and he had put his spoon in the lower section just like Graeme would have done. Graeme closed the dishwasher and went to get the corn flakes, but as he stood with the box in his hands he realised he wasn't hungry. Everyone has to eat, but he had no appetite, so he put the box back.

He stood at the bottom of the stairs and looked up. He could hear the other man's footsteps travel across the hall ceiling as their owner walked towards the bathroom. But then Graeme became aware of another set of footsteps—outside. The letter box clanged and a single envelope landed on the hall floor. In three quick strides, Graeme reached the front door, picked up the letter, noticing it bore his name, and stuffed it in his back pocket, then returned to the foot of the stairs. He climbed them quickly and quietly, becoming aware as he did so of the sound of the other man using the toilet. Graeme reached the top of the stairs, stepped on to the landing and looked into the bathroom. The other man had left the door open, which Graeme might also have done, but only if alone in the house. He—the other man—was standing in front of the toilet urinating and looking out of the window towards the backs of the houses beyond the rear garden. His stream diminished to a trickle, stopped, returned briefly, then stopped altogether. For a moment, the other man's legs bent forward slightly at the knee. Graeme moved towards the stairs that would take him up to the second floor. He managed to get out of sight before the other man had finished washing his hands.

Graeme risked a look back around the banisters. There was something lying on the carpet in the middle of the landing. He felt his back pocket. The letter wasn't there and now the other man was coming out of the bathroom. Graeme watched as the other man started to cross the landing and then stopped, his eye drawn to the letter on the carpet. The other man bent down and picked up the letter. He read the front and then turned the envelope over and tore it open.

He withdrew the contents, which comprised a single sheet of paper folded into three. He unfolded it, read it, folded it again and returned it to the envelope, and then he went back into the bedroom. Graeme listened to him moving around, opening and closing drawers. After a minute or two, the other man came out and went downstairs. Graeme heard a couple of doors being closed—the doors to the living room and kitchen—and then the other man put the alarm on and left the house, double-locking the front door.

Graeme waited a minute and then went downstairs. The alarm started beeping quietly, so he keyed in the code and it fell silent. In the kitchen, Graeme's keys were gone from their normal place. He helped himself to a spare pair and closed the kitchen door after him. Taking a jacket from the coat rack, he keyed in the alarm code and approached the front door. He turned the key in the lock and opened the door, stepping out into the fresh spring air.

There was no one at the bus stop, so Graeme sat and waited. The bus came and Graeme got on. He looked out of the window as the bus crawled through the student district and then entered an area dominated by Asian restaurants. When the bus reached the outskirts of the city centre Graeme got up and pressed the bell. The driver brought the bus to a halt and Graeme thanked him as he disembarked. He walked a short distance and entered the building where he worked. He crossed the atrium and climbed the spiral staircase. On the second floor he stepped inside the photocopy room and checked his pigeonhole, which was empty. He then proceeded along the corridor to his office.

Closing his fingers around the handle, he looked through the glass panel in the door. The other man was sitting at Graeme's desk running his finger under the flap of a self-sealed envelope. He turned to look towards the door and Graeme shrank back. He pressed his spine against the corridor wall and his knees gave a little. He allowed his back to slide down the wall, but then he heard the door to his office being opened from the inside. He immediately got to his feet, turned and walked away down the corridor. He had no way of knowing if the person opening the door was the other man or one of the colleagues with whom Graeme shared his office. He pushed open the double doors at the end of the corridor and once he reached the stairs he took them at a run.

Reaching the ground floor, Graeme crossed the atrium and left the building via the revolving door. He stopped immediately he was outside to recover his breath, but finding himself in the middle of a crowd of smokers he moved on.

Graeme started walking home. His route took him past Sarah's place of work. He went up to the sliding doors, which opened automatically, but then he backed away again and walked up and down on the pavement for two minutes. He took his mobile phone out of his pocket and looked at it. He found Sarah's number in the address book and his finger hovered over the call button, but then he cancelled it instead and put the phone away.

He walked home and when he got there he stood outside the house looking up at it. He checked his watch, waited a moment and then walked on. He walked beyond the shops, through the housing estate and past the rugby club and the allotments until he reached the river. It had not rained for a few days and the river was low. He walked on the path that followed the meander of the river. His watch told him it was lunchtime, but he was not hungry, even though he had had no breakfast.

Later in the afternoon, he returned home. He entered the house, switched off the alarm and went straight upstairs. He waited in the spare bedroom, from where he had a good view of the street. He watched one of his neighbours come out of her house and put a compostable bag of food waste in her green bin. She then picked up a confectionary wrapper from her front path and placed that in the regular dustbin before going back inside and closing the front door.

The other man walked up the road and approached the house. Graeme stepped back from the window and paced slowly across the floor. As he heard the front door being opened, he suddenly stopped and became aware of the exaggerated sound of his own breathing. He had not put the alarm on before coming upstairs. He stood absolutely still and listened. He heard the other man enter the kitchen and then move around the ground floor from room to room.

Graeme sat down, leaning against the wall. When he heard the front door again, he stood up.

"Hello-oo," Sarah called as her heels struck the wooden boards of the hall floor.

Graeme heard the other man respond and guessed he would be offering to make her a cup of tea. Taking care to minimise any noise, Graeme walked down to the first-floor landing and sat on the top step of the stairs that went down to the ground floor. Because of the half-landing and the one-hundred-and-eighty-degree turn, there was no way they could see him. He listened to them swop stories about their respective days. It sounded mechanical, listless, routine. He listened while they prepared food, poured wine, switched on the news.

When he heard Sarah coming upstairs he retreated to the next flight up before she reached the half-landing. Peering around the newel post he watched her enter the bathroom and listened to her using the toilet. She came out and stood for a moment on the landing. She looked tired. Maybe she was trying to remember if she had come upstairs for anything other than to go to the bathroom. Her face wore a strained expression. After a moment her facial muscles relaxed and she moved towards the stairs. Graeme gave it a few seconds before getting to his feet and taking an initial step to follow her, but then he stopped, staring at the spot on the landing where Sarah had been standing a moment earlier, and he raised his hands and ran them over his shaved head. He turned around and climbed the stairs back up to the top floor. He went into the spare bedroom and curled up on the bed.

Graeme awoke and looked around the unfamiliar room. At some point in the night he had got under the duvet, but he had not got undressed. His clothes were a bit crumpled, but they were not damp with sweat. He could hear noises from one floor down: one person in the bathroom, another moving around. He lay on his back and listened.

He became aware of footsteps leaving the bedroom, moving on to the landing, starting to climb the stairs. As quickly and quietly as he could, he got out of bed and stood by the door, eyes wide, senses alert. The approaching footsteps were light enough to be Sarah's, but it was hard to be sure. He looked around. The guest bedroom contained no hiding places. The footsteps stopped outside the door to the room. He held his breath.

The door opened slowly.

Sarah stood in the doorway.

From downstairs came the sound of the other man's voice.

"Have a nice day, darling."

Graeme looked at Sarah.

He could hear footsteps on the main stairs going down, a bracelet jangling, and then a voice—he would have said Sarah's voice—called from downstairs: "See you later."

The other man shouted back, "See you later."

Graeme took a step towards Sarah and looked into her eyes. He saw himself reflected in her pupils. But otherwise they looked empty.

The Blind Man

SIMISTER
POLEFIELD
PRESTWICH

As a young woman you took the trolleybus to work. Down Moston Lane it went, heading south, and when it turned left to go towards Collyhurst, the trolley would sometimes come off the wire. On those occasions you would be late for work and you would go in and you would say, "The trolley came off the wire." No one minded; everyone understood. The trolley came off the wire.

When you were saving up to marry my dad, you would walk the three miles instead. It took you just under an hour. You were a fast walker. You were never late for work then.

Once married, you and my dad moved to another part of the city and you caught the bus into town.

BAGULEY
MOSS SIDE
MANCHESTER

My dad didn't like you working, so you gave up the job. It was no hardship. You liked being at home. When I was a toddler, you would take me places on the bus. You used to leave the pushchair behind the stop. It was always there when we got back.

LANGLEY ROAD
PENDLETON
WEASTE

My dad worked long shifts at the docks. He expected his tea on the table when he got home. He got it, too. I discovered that I could alter the shape of the lines on his face by how loudly I cried for *my* tea. I knew that I created those lines and I could see they were directed not at me but at you.

ECCLES
PEEL GREEN
TRAFFORD PARK

I was ten when I started using the buses by myself and twelve when I began taking down their numbers and underlining them in a little orange book—*Fleetbook 1: Buses of Greater Manchester*. You could get other Fleetbooks in the Ian Allan shop on Piccadilly ramp. *Fleetbook 3: Buses of West Yorkshire*, which was turquoise. *Fleetbook 7: Buses of the East Midlands*—a drab green. *Fleetbook 15: Buses of Greater London*—grey, though I always thought it should have been red, because the Manchester one was orange, like our buses. But I couldn't afford them, the Fleetbooks. Not on my spends.

SWINTON
MONTON
ECCLES

I used to hear you and my dad rowing downstairs. You kept the door shut, but the sound came through the floorboards. I bent over my lists of numbers, looking for the buses I still needed, seeing which garages they were based at. I would fantasise about visiting them all. I wouldn't stop at Princess Road and Queens Road and Northenden. I would take the 400 to Rochdale and Oldham and Stockport. I would jump on the 263 or 264 to Altrincham.

It was from Altrincham garage that I took the blinds. They didn't let you go round the garages. It wasn't safe. So you had to creep in. I wrote down the numbers, breathed in the smell of diesel. I boarded the scrapped vehicles in the yard at the back. I unscrewed a bell-push. I helped myself to a square plastic information plate detailing the vehicle's dimensions. The metal trapdoor giving access to the housing for the destination blind was normally held in place by two catches: one of them was undone. I forced the other. The blind was easy to remove. I liberated a couple more from two tired old Crossleys and ended up having to run from the yard, a driver's angry cries ringing in my ears.

I hid the blinds at the back of my cupboard and I would take them out when there was no one else in the house and unroll them across the floor. I would read the names of places, some I had been to, others I would never see.

STALYBRIDGE
REDDISH
STOCKPORT

Somehow, you and my dad never came across the blinds, but my dad found the Fleetbooks in the hole in the wall I had made behind my desk. It was not quite a full set. I still needed *Fleetbook 13: Buses of Eastern Scotland.* They never had it in stock at Ian Allan's when I was shoplifting the others over a period of months.

Did you steal these?

No.

Are you a dirty little shoplifter?

No.

Did you steal them?

No.

Then why were they hidden in a hole behind your desk? A hole in the wall you vandalised for the purpose of hiding your dirty stolen goods. Tell the truth now, tell the truth and we'll forget all about it. The worst thing by far is lying about it. Tell the truth and you'll be forgiven. Did you steal them?

I looked at my dad. I saw you come up behind him, having been interrupted in your housework, a bottle of toilet cleaner in your hand. I couldn't read the expression on your face.

Yes, I said. I stole them.

You dirty little thieving bastard. You dirty little thief.

He took a step towards me, his face red, nostrils flaring. I saw him draw back his hand and I flinched. But, with his hand raised, he turned away from me and pointed a finger in your face. What did he mean? That it was your fault? That you would pay for it later? I never saw him hit you, but there was a violence in him.

You stepped into the space he had vacated and now your face resembled his. Your arm came up in a sudden movement. Either you squeezed the plastic bottle or momentum brought the blue liquid sloshing out of the spout, and the world became a blue film that quickly faded to black.

BELLE VUE
AUDENSHAW
NORTH MANCHESTER GENERAL HOSPITAL

My dad burned the Fleetbooks, but I kept the blinds, carrying them from one foster home to another, where they stayed rolled up for most of the time. In the middle of the night—it was all the same to me—I would get them out and unroll them and run my fingers over the smooth canvas, believing I could still read the white letters against the black. And when I finally got my own place, I hung them on the walls. It made the room darker, but that didn't matter to me. I would invite people round and ask them to read them to me.

RADCLIFFE
BESSES O' TH' BARN
PENDLEBURY

Finally, I invited you. I assured you that if I had been angry, I was no longer. You can't remain angry for ever. You came. I invited you in and you entered and sat down. Like any visitor, you were asked if you would read to me from the walls.

SALE MOOR
BROOKLANDS
SOUTHERN CEMETERY

Sitting Tenant

Mark and Elinore had been in the rented house six months. It felt more like twelve. Every day, Mark cruised the estate agents in the village. He knew everybody's name and they knew his, but that didn't make houses come on to the market any faster. If people weren't looking to move, familiarity with the estate agents was irrelevant. Not that one or two hadn't gone out of their way to make sure he heard about houses that sounded like the kind of thing they were looking for. But they were always too small. Or too modern. Or too expensive. Or there was no off-street parking. Or the garden was overlooked, or too poky, or it faced north.

The estate agents didn't help, with their wide-angle photographs that made back yards look like national parks, and their brochures so full of spin they fanned out on the coffee table all by themselves. "The house is adjacent to Fog Lane Park." Really? When you get there, you see there's actually another house between the park and the house you're viewing. "The house is adjacent to Marie Louise Gardens." Can it be true? No, it's not, it's across the street.

"Look at this," Mark said to Elinore over breakfast. "'The garden has a southerly aspect.' You know what that means."

"I imagine it faces east," said Elinore. "I'm going to be late."

In the other room, the kids were bickering. Thomas was winding up Caitlin. Mark swore and got to his feet. He went in the other room and shouted at them. Thomas answered back and Mark felt a sudden, almost uncontrollable compulsion to belt him. Instead he returned to the kitchen.

"I wish you wouldn't shout at them so much," she said.

"They don't take any notice otherwise."

"You're turning into your father."

"Whom you never met. All you know about him is what I've told you."

"Yeah, well. Exactly. I've got to go."

He watched her cross the tiny kitchen, grinding her teeth. The stress, the frustration, the endless series of disappointments. It was getting to her.

"Didn't your folks live round here at some point?" Elinore asked him that night once the kids were in bed and they were preparing dinner.

"Yeah, I've got all the addresses written down somewhere. Prices were reasonable then. Pass me that steamer."

"Before or after they broke up? Don't overdo the vegetables for once."

"After. Can you imagine a single person finding a place in Didsbury now? Anything with its own front door, I mean. If you want your veg raw, by the way, eat them straight from the pack. I'm cooking mine."

Later, the argument not so much forgotten as cautiously accommodated, Mark and Elinore were in bed.

He took the newspaper out of her hands and let it slide on to the floor. Elinore's dressing gown was lying on the bed. He unthreaded the cord and used it to tie her right hand to the bedstead.

"This wasn't as straightforward before," Mark said.

"No?" she said.

"Well, our own bed may be more comfortable than this one, but it has nothing up here you can tie anything to."

"Still, it's the one thing I'm most looking forward to getting out of storage when we finally find a house."

He reached for his own dressing gown and liberated its cord, which he used to secure Elinore's left hand, then he pulled the quilt back. She pressed her head back into the pillow, closing her eyes. He leaned over.

Mark received a text from one of the agents. Four-bed Cheshire semi, good-sized garden.

He called and made an appointment.

He looked at the map. The name of the road was familiar and he couldn't work out why.

They liked it. They liked it enough to see it a second time.

"Do you know much about the neighbours?" Mark asked the estate agent.

"Absentee landlords," the young woman replied. "The house is rented out. Some of the time it's empty. Look, have a think. I'll be outside."

"We'll have to move fast if we don't want to lose it," Mark said to Elinore.

"Yes, but, Mark, we have to make sure it's the right place."

By now they were standing in the back garden.

Mark had remembered why the name of the street was familiar, but he hadn't told Elinore. She'd only say he was letting his heart rule his head.

"There's an outhouse," she said.

"It looks recent. Relatively, I mean."

Would they or wouldn't they?

She had to be the one to say it.

"Shall we?" she asked him.

"What do you think?"

"I think we should."

And so they did.

The first night in the new house, Mark bathed the children. He washed Caitlin's hair, then sat her on a chair in the middle of her new bedroom to dry it. He stood behind her with the hairdryer like a hairdresser.

"Are you going anywhere nice this year, madam?" he asked her, pulling a brush through her velvety hair.

"Daddy, don't be silly. I'm not going anywhere," she answered him firmly.

Being in the new place didn't begin to feel weird until the kids were in bed.

"They're excited being in a new place," Elinore said.

He heard a knocking. One of the kids, perhaps. They were probably still awake.

"What was that?" Elinore asked.

He looked at her, faintly annoyed that she'd thought it worth mentioning. That it had been allowed to disturb their evening. He turned to stare at the blank screen of the TV.

"I don't know. One of the kids."

"I don't think so. Maybe it was someone at the door."

"It wasn't anyone at the door."

He looked at Elinore again. Her legs tucked up on the settee. Glass of Shiraz on the stripped floor just within reach. So what? She was the one who went out to work. Stressful job, proper salary. He stayed at home, worked freelance.

He walked into the hall. He could see through the stained glass that there was no one at the door. He wandered into the front room. No furniture, just stacks and stacks of boxes separated by narrow aisles. He felt like a giant walking into Manhattan.

The knocking could have been coming from anywhere.

He stood in the bay window and looked down the street, wondering which house had been his father's. It could have been this one, but it could just as easily have been any one of the others. He hadn't been able to find the list of old addresses his mother had helped him compile. Possibly it was at the bottom of one of the boxes behind him.

He heard a voice floating down from the top of the stairs.

"Mummy . . . Daddy."

"I'll go, Elinore," he said.

He found Thomas and Caitlin sitting side by side on the top step.

"What's the matter?" he asked.

"We can hear noises."

"It's just the house. Come on, back to bed. I'll tuck you up. Chop chop."

The following morning, Mark put a load of washing on and stood looking out of the kitchen window. It occurred to him that they didn't have a washing line.

As he was pulling the front door to, he heard a knocking sound similar to the noise they had heard the night before.

The village was quiet. In the hardware shop, Mark asked about a washing line. The man produced one from a shelf. Mark picked it up. He liked the feel of the cool plastic on his skin.

"I'll take two, please."

He walked back up Wilmslow Road, passed by buses of every colour all operating the same route but charging different fares. He remembered when he was growing up in Altrincham, the buses were all orange and white, and a small yellow square ticket that would take you all the way to Piccadilly cost you 2p.

When he got home, he put one of the washing lines up in the back garden and took the other one up to their bedroom. He opened his bedside drawer and dropped it in.

Mark spent the rest of the day unpacking boxes, then played with the kids in the back garden. He was lying on his back on the lawn with both children climbing on top of him when Elinore came home. Playfully he pushed them off and went to pour her a glass of wine, and crack open a beer.

They sat with their drinks at the end of the garden.

"Have you heard that knocking today?" asked Elinore.

"Elinore, behold the idyllic scene. Don't spoil it. No, I haven't heard it."

But they heard it that night.

"Maybe it's the neighbours," Mark suggested, turning down the TV.

"Didn't the agent say it was empty?"

"Look, we've finally got a lovely house. And we're surrounded by all our own stuff again. We should be able to relax now. Don't worry about a little noise."

Elinore stared at the TV, grinding her teeth.

"Will you put up that mirror in the hall tomorrow?" she said.

"Whatever you want. I want us to be happy here."

In the morning, Mark found himself up a ladder in the hall with a drill, a pocketful of Rawl plugs and a mouthful of language.

"Fucking Rawl plugs. Fucking stupid bastard Rawl plugs."

The wall was like a slab of Emmental. Each hole had a Rawl plug either sticking out of it or jammed so far in it was equally useless.

Mark got down off the ladder and called Elinore.

"It doesn't seem to matter what size Rawl plug I use, what size drill bit and what size screw, it's completely impossible to match them up."

"You're only putting a mirror up."

"It's quite a big mirror. Hang on. There's someone knocking. I've got to go."

He opened the front door, but there was no one there.

Mark scratched his head. He went round the house checking in every cupboard, behind all the doors, for a dangling coathanger or loose hinge. He shone a torch in the darkest corners of the cellar and climbed up into the eaves, but found nothing that might be the source of the noise. In the end, putting the mirror up began to seem like light relief, so he got back up the ladder and drilled another hole. He slotted the Rawl plug in. It still didn't go in all the way, so he pulled the hammer out of his belt and gave it a whack.

The Rawl plug disappeared into the hole, which itself suddenly expanded dramatically as a section of plaster collapsed and fell inside.

Mark swore.

A cold draught wafted out of the hole.

Mark moved his body closer to the wall and put his eye to the hole.

It was too dark. He got the torch and, with the plaster around the edge of the hole crumbling beneath his touch, pointed its feeble beam into the darkness within.

Mark looked back at the hole from the other side. It was bigger now. A lot bigger. Big enough to climb through.

He was in a room. Not a big room, maybe eight foot by twelve. In the middle of the room was a chair, a standard wooden kitchen chair. And on the chair were the remains of a young woman.

He knew it was a woman because of the jewellery. Simple, inexpensive pieces. A ring, a necklace. Her wrists were tied to the chair behind her back with a length of grimy plastic-coated washing line. It was evident the room had been sealed a long time ago. Years rather than months.

Shock made Mark's entire body shake as he circled the chair. His face had become cold. He put a hand up to his cheeks. They were wet. He knelt in a corner of the room, his torch beam picking out the dead girl's skull, while he chewed the inside of his mouth.

He forced himself to have another close look, in case there were any obvious sign of how she had met her death. There wasn't. He couldn't stop himself imagining scenarios. The girl tied to the chair in the middle of the room. A man behind her, perhaps holding a hood that he would force over her head. Maybe he would have circled her like Mark had just done. If she was conscious, she might have pleaded for her life. He might have hit her. He might have crouched down in the corner and cried.

Mark fixed up the hole in the wall as best he could, then hung the mirror over it.

He sat in the back garden, thinking. The outhouse, he realised, had been added to conceal the presence of the hidden room from anyone using the garden.

The bedroom above the hidden room was Caitlin's. He remembered sitting her on a chair in the middle of the room to dry her hair. He would have to swop with her and make that room his studio.

That night, once the kids had gone to bed, Mark and Elinore sat in front of the TV.

Mark had not managed to find the list of his father's old addresses. He'd looked, half-heartedly, in a couple of boxes, then abandoned the search.

"I want you to be happy here," Mark said, during the ads.

"We will be," said Elinore, with a little smile.

"It's you and the children I'm thinking about," he said quietly. "I don't want anything to go wrong."

He looked at the wall and thought about what was on the other side of it. He thought about what he'd done, or rather hadn't done, and whether it was the right thing. He didn't feel he'd had a choice. He listened throughout the evening, but didn't hear the knocking sound again.

The Trees

I was pleased with the way it had gone, introducing Jane to my parents, though I wasn't sure for whose benefit we'd done it. Probably Jane's first, then theirs and mine last. I wanted them to meet her all right, no question about that, but I'd sensed how impatient they were with the fact that I was nearing thirty and still single and I didn't want the symbolism of the meeting to get too heavy. Jane and I had only been together a few months. Still, I felt okay about the direction in which we seemed to be heading.

So we drove the ninety miles to the coast in Jane's clapped-out old Austin Maxi. My parents had moved to a permanently damp port on the east side of the country. About the only thing that remained dry there was my Dad's sense of humour.

"Have you still not got a job then?" he asked me once the introductions were over. I worked full time as a draughts-man, but in a freelance capacity for a number of different companies, and my Dad, now that he was retired, worried full time on my behalf.

When I was younger I'd always thought that by the age of thirty I'd be an adult, in charge of all my own affairs, with no one around to approve or disapprove. But I guess your parents are always your parents, whatever age you are, and in one sense at least, you remain a child as long as they're alive.

Jane had been a little nervous, but the whole thing went off perfectly well. They seemed to take a genuine liking to her, and the three of them chatted easily while I withdrew from the room on the pretext of visiting the toilet. I hadn't told Jane they'd also met my last two girlfriends and liked them, because she would probably have felt under even more pressure. "I'm getting a bit tired of meeting your girlfriends and getting to know them," Mum had said to me, quite reasonably, "and then you finish with them."

I went upstairs and had a quick look in the bathroom and my parents' bedroom. It's just something I do whenever I go to see family or friends: I always have a bit of a look round. I spotted a couple of pictures on the dresser that hadn't been there last time I had. One showed the whole family squinting into the sun on a walking holiday in the Lakes, the other my Dad on top of a mountain somewhere in Wales. I held the first photograph up to my eye and studied Mum's and Dad's faces, faces I'd known for thirty years, but these days I only saw them every eight weeks or so, if that. When they'd opened the door to us that night I'd registered instantly that my Dad's hair had more grey in it and my Mum's, behind that lifelong familiarity, was clearly getting older as well. But it's like taking two steps forward and one step back: having noticed that two-month change, suddenly I saw them as Mum and Dad again, same as they always were. After all, the age difference between us would never change.

I looked at the photograph, remembering the holiday as clearly as if it were yesterday, the curdling mix of butter and cucumber, and the quick pain of scratching a sunburnt arm. But also the excitement of spotting lizards before they darted between the cracks in stone walls, the satisfaction of building a dam of stones across the ghyll. The memories were luxurious but they hurt at the same time: the heart full of hope and the mind so aware of the inevitability of passing time.

I didn't want my parents to get any older. I didn't know how I'd cope. I couldn't even think about it.

I took a right turn off the main road and rolled the Maxi down to a little crossroads.

"Which way is it?" Jane asked, leaning forward to peer through the windscreen at the faded wooden signs. It was about ten in the evening now, middle of February, and it had already been going dark when we'd arrived at my parents' at around 5:30. After dinner—my Mum had cooked my favourites: meat and potato pie with red cabbage, followed by lemon meringue pie—I'd suggested a drive up the coast to have a look round what remained of the village of Speedwell.

"I've got these pots to do," my Mum had said.

"I'll do them," I told her.

"No, I'll do them and your Dad'll dry. I always do them. You know that."

I did, it was true: she never let anyone do the dishes. Sometimes, as a boy, I'd washed my own supper pots—a coffee mug and a side plate—but that was all. She said no one else could wash them without breaking things and, as far as I could remember, she'd never actually broken anything herself.

"You two go," Mum said, and I realised she was giving us the opportunity to have some time together.

So we drove up the main road thirty miles or so to the Speedwell turn-off. Jane sat in the passenger seat—she liked having me drive even though it was her car; my old thing was currently the centre of attention at Eric's Escort Agency—and we chatted about this and that. She fiddled with the digital dial on the radio—a new acquisition after Jane's last job painting stage scenery in Croydon—and she managed to lose all the wavelengths I'd programmed in for her.

"Sorry," she said with a little smile when button two produced a tangle of Dutch instead of Radio 4.

"It's your radio," I said, going left at the crossroads.

"Yes, but you'll have to programme it again."

True, and I didn't mind, but we fell silent for a few minutes. We were at a stage in our relationship where we could *almost* take such silences for granted and not notice them. But I, at least, was still slightly conscious of the gaps.

"Are those what your Dad gave you?" she asked, looking at my shoes.

Before dinner my Dad had dug out some of his unused work boots, those with steel toe caps. He didn't need them any more, he'd said, and we both wore the same size. The boots rubbed slightly, but I liked their sturdy, heavy feel on my feet.

"Thanks a lot," I'd said as he got down on his hands and knees looking for more unwanted stuff in his wardrobe. "You've still got that old thing," I said, spotting one of his Michael Caine sports jackets.

"You can have that as well if you want," he offered, emerging with another pair of shoes.

Why was he giving me all this stuff? Did he think he wasn't going to live much longer? It struck me that however much he worried about it—and he had a list of imaginary ailments as long as my arm—he was in fact fit and well and could easily be around for another thirty-odd years. In other words, until I was as old as he was now.

Then I thought of Mum downstairs preparing the dinner with her hands caught in the slow grip of arthritis. I knew she fretted about the possibility of it getting worse. She was always active, never let her hands rest, as if she feared they might seize up in an idle moment.

I took the boots but put the jacket back.

"Yes," I said to Jane. "They're good, aren't they?"

"Very nice."

We passed a sign warning of deer—a stag with antlers in a red triangle—and I drove on towards Speedwell. I'd visited the village once before, but in daylight. Most of the village was supposed to have fallen into the sea at some point in the distant past and there was talk of being able to hear its former inhabitants moaning in the wind when the tide was low. I had a particular reason, which I hadn't mentioned to Jane, for wanting to see the place again and at night. A colleague at one of the firms where I'd been working had mentioned the village and I'd asked him what he knew about the place.

"I'll tell you later," he said, gesturing at his drawing board.

So I caught up with him later the same day in the office kitchen. People came in and out to make mugs of disgusting lukewarm instant coffee and, like Clive, to light up because the office was non-smoking. He was a man of curious contrasts: a well-groomed, just-so sort of man with an eye-catching green Zeiss coating on the lenses of his glasses, and yet he was never without a pack of twenty B&H in his top pocket. I mean, if he was going to smoke at all, you would have expected Gauloises or Gitanes—or Capstan Full Strength for that matter—but he chose common-as-muck Bensons.

He offered me the pack. That was the other thing about Clive: the most forgetful man I'd ever met. I shook my head.

He just closed the lid and replaced the pack in his shirt pocket. Apart from having a head like a sieve he was one of the most down-to-earth people I knew, which meant that his story made all the more of an impression on me.

"I went there with Helen," he said, leaning back against the sink. "I was driving. It was late, I don't know what time, but it was quite dark. I don't know if you know, but there's only two roads to Speedwell, both going off the main road."

I nodded. "We just wanted to have a look at the village because we'd heard about it. But we never actually got to see it." He inhaled and plucked the cigarette from between his lips with forefinger and thumb. "We were driving down this little road and there were trees either side in regular lines. I had the full beam on because there were no other cars. And gradually the trees started to arc overhead, over the road. Within about fifty yards they'd formed a tight canopy above the road, and the effect of my lights . . . I don't know . . . something . . . made me feel frightened." He sucked on his cigarette again, producing a hissing sound as the air was pulled through it. "Suddenly I became really frightened and I couldn't explain it at all. There was just the canopy of trees and the way the headlights were caught.

"I looked at Helen—we didn't speak, didn't say a word, either of us—and I stopped the car, turned around and drove back to the main road."

He sipped his coffee, then put it down on the sink and folded his arms. "The strangest thing was we didn't say a word and yet we both felt it. Helen told me later she felt it as well."

The fields stretched out on either side of the road, but we couldn't see more than a few yards because it was so dark. You could just make out furrowed soil and the occasional shock of hedgerow. There was a blustery wind which buffeted the car and made us feel quite isolated, as if *it* was part of the land and we weren't, and it was trying to blow us back to wherever we belonged.

I'd seen those M. R. James adaptations on television when I was a kid and been affected by them. He'd written about this part of the world and made it frightening. Or more likely, it seemed to me, looking out on to the grim fields, he'd just picked up on what was here already. If any part of the country looked as if it might spawn little demons and evil creatures to scamper across the road, a blur in the headlights, this was surely it.

Then the trees started appearing.

I glanced at Jane. Her seat was pushed back, meaning I had to turn to see her. She was playing with the radio, with her toes. She must have hit two buttons at the same time—a station and the volume control—because suddenly a din erupted in the back of the car. It sounded like grunge played backwards or punk at the wrong speed. Anyway, it made me wince, and Jane found the off switch with her hand, looking at me sheepishly.

"Radio 4 again," she said, drawing her knees up under her chin. For some strange reason of her own she never wore a safety belt. I'd tried to convince her it was a good idea but she had a face she pulled for times like that—whenever I tried to tell her what to do—and it never failed to put me in my place.

More trees sprang up along the side of the narrow road, my headlights picking out their trunks from the darkness like skittles. I slowed down slightly and wondered if I was going to feel anything or if Clive's story would prove to be no more than just that. Within seconds the trees formed unbroken lines on both sides of the road and the light from the car caught both walls of foliage as if they were of far solider stuff.

A brief chill tickled the back of my neck and I realised with a guilty flush of excitement that I was picking up something of Clive's inexplicable terror.

The trees arched overhead, branches interweaving. The trapped light made it seem like we were in a tunnel.

Now I did feel frightened. I shivered involuntarily and felt my arms prickle with goosepimples, but I kept my foot on the accelerator. This would have been the moment when Clive had turned round. I sneaked a quick look at Jane.

She was white, eyes like drops of ink on a sheet of blotting paper, her mouth hanging open.

My hands tightened on the wheel to compensate for my arms, which had gone slack. Something penetrated my stomach with its cold fist and then opened its fingers like someone waking up. My whole body trembled, spidery sweat crawling out from my hairline.

Still the tunnel unrolled before the car, uninterrupted, and I felt my slick palms begin to slip on the wheel. Suddenly the walls broke, the trees fell away and the light escaped into the night once more. A house came up on the left, and a choice of two even narrower roads. I took the beach road and seconds later ground the car to a halt in the gravel of the car park.

We sat there without speaking. Jane turned and looked at me but I couldn't face her. I knew I'd had no right to do that with her in the car unwarned about what to expect. I didn't know what to say to her. Then I heard her door open and shut and watched her walk in front of the car down towards the beach, her arms wrapped around her body for protection against the bitter wind. I sighed. How stupid I'd been.

It had certainly been frightening though. Clive had been right. But more frightening than I'd bargained for and the adventure now seemed pretty silly.

I got out of the car and followed the path Jane had taken to the beach. At first I couldn't see where she'd got to. Then I saw her standing a few yards from the incoming waves, staring out to sea, her beautiful long brown hair blowing in the wind like a scarf. I scrunched through the pebbles to get to her and came alongside a few feet from where she stood. She didn't turn, but after a few moments she did speak.

"It's quite scary down here as well, isn't it? I mean, a beach at night. It's not somewhere you tend to go after dark."

I nodded and made a kind of non-committal murmur. There were no ships' lights and you couldn't make out the horizon, so even though you thought you knew where it would be, there was a wedge of impenetrable darkness instead between the sea and the star-flecked sky.

"Where are the remains of the village supposed to be then?" Jane asked. I found her neutral tone disturbing.

"Straight out from here," I said, trying to sound interested because she'd asked the question rather than because I cared about the legend.

"You almost expect to see a church steeple sticking up through the waves," she said quietly.

The cold bit through my thick woollen coat. "I'm going back to the car," I said. "Are you coming?"

"In a minute."

I trudged back over the pebbles. There were some anglers a hundred yards away, storm lamps glowing behind their big green umbrellas. I could see them standing in a huddle to one side and part of me envied them their camaraderie. I imagined a catch was unlikely on a night like this but that the fish were less important to them than just being there together.

I got in the car and started the engine to warm it up before Jane reappeared. The interior light was not working and I peered at the road map by the feeble light of the car park's single lamp to check our way back. I heard footsteps and Jane's door being opened so I stuffed the map in the door pocket and turned to watch her get in.

"Are you okay?" I asked.

"Let's go," she said. She looked straight ahead and said nothing else.

I turned the car round and we rolled out of the car park, past the Stag Inn, where there were lights burning. I thought about asking Jane if she fancied a drink but it didn't seem like a good idea in the current climate—decidedly chilly. I flicked the stalk to cast more light on the road ahead. The little blue light that came on to indicate the full beam was some comfort: whatever car I was driving, the blue light always reminded me of the old Jaguar my Dad had driven us around in when I was a child. On long journeys at night I'd occasionally stir and peer over the front seats at the dashboard. It intrigued me to see the blue light go on and off as other cars emerged out of the darkness, then passed us and disappeared again. I asked my Dad what the blue light meant, but because I was too small to understand how you could possibly alter the headlamps by switching a blue light on and off, the little blue spot assumed magical qualities. My Dad used it to get us safely home.

My Mum was in on it too. I used to poke my head round her seat next to the door and she'd say "Hello sunshine" and smile at me. Then I'd curl up and go back to sleep.

There was no one in the back now, but in a sense there was no need because the child was still inside me. The blue light meant the same to me now as it had then. My skin went cold at the idea of it going out for good.

Jane's voice made me jump. "Why did you want to come here?"

"What do you mean?" I said. "Look, what's wrong, Jane? What've I done?"

"I asked you a question. Why did you want to come here?" Her voice was as cold as the air inside the car had become.

"I wanted to introduce you to my parents. You did keep asking me if I would, after all."

"I mean here," she snapped. "Speedwell."

I thought about telling her the truth. We were coming up to where the road was bound on both sides by the trees. In two seconds we'd be in that tunnel of pale light again.

"Someone at work was going on about it," I said as the trees sprang to attention on either side of us, their thin, lower branches whipping about in the wind.

Jane's voice rose. "Saying what about it?"

"Saying I should go there."

"You'd already been there."

"It sounded like it'd be worth coming back."

We kept the truth in the air between us, batting it to and fro, neither of us daring to catch it, and the temperature in the car dropped through the floor. The light was pressed back at us by the trees, on both sides and overhead. I was shaking. Jane's voice trembled as she pressed me for more.

"What did this someone say about it?"

"That it was frightening. They turned back." There, I'd said it.

"We didn't though, did we? And you didn't tell me. I let you drive because I thought I could trust you."

She stopped as the trees receded behind the car. Without realising it, I'd been putting my foot down and we were hurtling towards the crossroads. The car flew across, so now I'd missed the right turn back to the main road, and, rather than stop and turn round, it seemed easier to carry on through the other little villages and catch up with the main road further south.

"I'm sorry, Jane," I said, then glanced at her. She was staring straight ahead, her mouth a pencil stroke. It scared me to see her like that—I dreaded confrontation—so I faced the front and just drove. At the next crossroads I went straight on, then had to choose at the next junction between the road ahead, which looked more like a track, or a left turn, which seemed to take us away from the direction we wanted to go in but was at least a proper road. Two hundred yards later at another junction I had to concede we were lost. I took the map from the pocket and held it up to my face, but I couldn't see anything by the light of the dash. With the interior light not working and there not being any torch as far as I knew—and I didn't want to risk further confrontation by asking Jane—the only thing for it was to take the map outside and read it by the light of the headlamps.

I muttered something to the effect of what I was doing and opened my door. The wind grabbed the door from my hand and then caught me by the hair. There was a row of trees next to the road being tugged this way and that. Somewhere beyond them I could hear the distant thrumming of hooves on packed earth. I went to the front of the car and bent down over the map. I felt so stupid to have treated Jane the way I had. She deserved better than that.

It wasn't altogether clear from the map, because it was small scale and couldn't show all the tiny little roads, but it seemed as if a right turn might be the best option from where we were.

I stood up, and, deliberately not looking at Jane through the windscreen, walked back to the driver's door. I noticed I'd left it open and again felt stupid for having let her get cold. But when I got into my seat and closed the door it seemed a lot warmer than it had been. Without turning to look at Jane I released the clutch and spun the wheel to the right. The road looked similar to the one that led into Speedwell, though we couldn't possibly have described a complete circle. A line of trees approached on the right, bent almost double by the wind. There was a strange smell in the car which I presumed I'd brought in from outside, and I was so angry with myself and worked up I was getting hotter by the second. We tore along the road which was now lined on both sides by trees. The blue full-beam light flicked on and off as the car hit bumps in the road, and when I tried the stalk to see what was wrong, it flapped loosely in my hand. It was becoming unbearably hot in the car and I couldn't stand the silent treatment any longer. I glanced at Jane out of the corner of my eye, saw just a flash of red and turned my head to get a proper look.

I screamed and the wheel jerked out of my hands. The car skidded and thumped into the grass verge. Jane's throat had been opened and there was blood down the front of her clothes. I felt the heat coming off her. And the smell had got much worse, like the stench of an animal. My stomach turned itself inside out, my body convulsing. I felt something hot on the back of my neck and raised my eyes a fraction to see in the rear-view mirror.

It was dark back there but I could just make out a mask of barely human features and above it, silhouetted against the back window, through which the trees stood waving in the wind, the twist and curve of antlers.

Hide and Seek

It was a way to pass the time and keep the kids happy. Kids. When I was a kid myself I didn't like the word. I didn't like being referred to as one of "the kids". It seemed unrespectful, dismissive. I preferred to be one of "the children". When my own kids were born, I consequently referred to them always as "the children", never "the kids". In fact, to qualify that, it was when the first one was born that I stuck religiously to that rule, which lasted until just after the second one came along. The second and final one, I might add. Nothing I've ever done in my life drains the energy quite like having kids. Don't get me wrong: I wouldn't go back. I wouldn't un-have them. My life has been enriched—immeasurably. Practically anyone who's had kids will tell you the same. Apart from the abusers, the loveless, the miserable. So no, I wouldn't go back, but nor would I have any more. I'm shattered as it is; plus, how could I love another one as much as I adore the two I've got? Mind you, I thought that after the birth of the first one.

Harry, our first-born, is a handful, as naughty as he is adorable. Good as an angel one minute, absolute horror the next. Would I have him any other way? The standard answer is no. I wouldn't want him any different. The standard answer sucks, however. Doesn't take a genius to work that one out. Sure I'd have him different. I'd have him good all the time. It would make life easier, that's all. However, he's lovable the way he is and if making him any less naughty made him any less lovable, then, no, I wouldn't have him any different.

He's funny. He makes faces and strikes poses I wouldn't have thought a four-year-old capable of. He's a mimic in the making. I love him like—well, there is no like. I love him more than anything or anyone I've ever loved. Before his sister came long. Now I love her the same way I love him. I'm nuts about her. If our relationship is less developed, less complex than the relationship I have with Harry, that's only because he's got two years' head start. Our dialogue is less sophisticated, but we still talk. In fact she's talking more and more all the time. For months, while other two-year-olds were chattering away, Sophie remained silent. She'd point and she'd cry, but she didn't have much vocab. Then it started to come in a rush. Now she knows words I didn't know she knew. Every day she surprises me with another one. The longest sentence she can speak gets longer every day. She's also the most beautiful little girl you've ever seen (takes after her mum—my wife—Sally), but then they all say that.

Sometimes when I'm out with the two of them some-where I forget that while Harry's walking beside me and holding my hand, Sophie's sitting on my shoulders, and I briefly slip into a dizzying panic. Where is she? Where have I left her? Will I ever see her again? Sure you will, she's sitting on your shoulders. It's like forgetting you're wearing your glasses. Don't tell me you've never done that: searched for your glasses for a good quarter of an hour, only to realise eventually they're stuck on the front of your head.

But those moments, those moments when I forget she's there and I don't know where she is, they remind me of when Harry was little. I mean really little, three months or so. When having a baby was still a novelty, when you turned round and saw him lying in his Moses basket and gave a little start because you'd forgotten, you'd forgotten you'd got a kid—or a child.

I had this fear that one day I'd look in the Moses basket and he wouldn't be there. Not that he could climb or roll out of it, he couldn't, but that he just wouldn't be there. That somehow I would have reverted to that pre-parental state. Gone backwards at speed. One minute I had a child, the next minute I didn't. It didn't make any sense, of course, but a lot of stuff goes through your head in those early months that doesn't make any sense.

I was looking after both the kids. Sally was working late, attending a meeting. Harry kept going on about Agnes, one of his little friends. He wanted her to come round. Or to go round to hers. We couldn't do that, I explained, because Agnes's parents had invited us round to theirs the other day. You have to be invited, I explained to him. You can't invite yourself.

Agnes's parents were our closest friends and they lived just two streets away. To stop Harry going on about it, I called them to invite them over. It turned out Agnes's mum, Siobhan, was at the same meeting Sally was at. They worked in the same field. So Agnes's dad, William, was looking after Agnes on his own. Looks like the tables have been turned, he joked. Our wives are out at work and we're left holding the babies.

Then he explained he was trying to finish some work of his own and needed to make the most of Siobhan's being out at the meeting. He was going to try to get Agnes into bed early. Instead, I offered to look after Agnes while he got on with his work. I'll bring her back after an hour or so, I said. Are you sure? he asked. No problem, I said. She's a very easy child.

William dropped Agnes round and she ran into the house, all excited at spending time with Harry and Sophie. William called after her, hoping for a goodbye kiss or hug before he went back home, but she was gone. I saw his crestfallen face, knew how he felt, but knew also that he'd be feeling relieved to have offloaded Agnes for a bit, so he'd be able to get some work done, or just have a break. I locked the door after him: my kids knew about not leaving the house unattended, and no doubt Agnes did too, but it didn't pay to be careless. So there I was now with three of them to keep happy at least until Sally got home. No problem, I'd said to William. No problem, I thought to myself. I loved Agnes almost like my own. Almost. There's always that almost. The love you have for your own kids is different. It's instinctive, fiercely protective. With someone else's kids it's less visceral, more of an affectionate responsibility.

Let's play hide and seek, I suggested. Yes! they all shouted, jumping up and down. Hide and seek. Hide and seek.

Who wants to hide first? I asked. Me! they chorused.

When Harry first started playing hide and seek, when he was two and a half, perhaps, or three, he'd tell you where he was going to hide. I'm going to hide under the bed, he'd say, and you'd try to explain why that wasn't really going to work. Later he would just close his eyes, believing that if he closed his eyes, not only could he not see you, but you couldn't see him either. Eventually he got the hang of it and became quite proficient at the game. He got so that you genuinely couldn't find him for two or three minutes. It was pretty much the only time, apart from when he was asleep, that you could get him to keep still and quiet for more than ten seconds. For this reason we encouraged the playing of hide and seek.

Sophie was still only learning, like Harry had been at her age. And Agnes—well, I was about to find out how good Agnes was at hide and seek.

Who's going to hide first? I asked, as if I didn't know. All three shouted "Me!" and put their hands up, but I knew from experience that if it wasn't Harry, then it wasn't going to work. He'd go into a sulk, wouldn't play properly and everything would start to fall apart. Okay, Harry first, I said, raising my arms and my voice to forestall protest. The rest of us count to ten.

Twenty, he shouted as he bounded up the stairs.

I counted loudly enough to drown out his retreat and the girls joined in. Sophie was jumping up and down with excitement. She had just learned how to jump and liked to do it as much as possible whenever there was a situation that seemed to call for it. Twenty, we concluded at the tops of our voices. Coming ready or not. Dead silence from the rest of the house. That's my boy.

Shall we look in the kitchen first, I suggested, in case he managed to sneak past us while we had our eyes shut?

The girls both nodded and I led the way into the kitchen, which smelled of onions and fried minced lamb. Still steaming on the hob was the big pan of chilli I'd made earlier for Sally and me to enjoy in front of the TV when the kids were in bed. The fridge door was a collage of art postcards, Bob the Builder yoghurt magnets and photo booth pictures of me and Sally with the kids. Over in the corner, a stereo was playing Porcupine Tree's *Lightbulb Sun* album for about the twenty-third time that day.

No sign of him here, I said. Shall we look in the dining room?

The knocked-through dining room and lounge looked like it usually did when both kids had been home for more than half an hour. Like a cyclone had ripped through the boxes, crates and cupboards filled with toys. A riot of Thomas the Tank Engine, Buzz Lightyear and Woody, Teletubbies and Barbie. Scott Tracey and Lady Penelope masks. Bob the Builder construction vehicles. Britains models and Matchbox Superfast cars (handed down from father to son). Teddy bears, rag dolls and dozens of assorted soft toys. Full marks to the kids for having out-Chapmanned the Chapman Brothers, who would have been proud of the maelstrom of miscegenation and mutilation.

No sign of him here either, I said, checking under the coffee table and behind the settee. Shall we look upstairs?

Yes!

Upstairs we looked in Sophie's room. We'd recently taken the side off her cot. As a result she could get out of bed and wander in the night, which was marginally preferable to one of us having to go to her if she started crying. Let her come to us instead.

Harry wasn't in Sophie's room.

Sophie and Agnes had already checked out the bathroom. Next was Harry's room. Harry had recently become keen on colouring in and cutting out and sticking down. His masterpieces covered every available inch of wall space. On the floor was a little pile of jagged scraps of paper from his most recent session with the kiddie-proof scissors. I quickly looked under his bed, but could only see his plastic Ikea toy crate-on-castors that I knew was full of dressing-up gear, Batman costumes, old scarves and so on. He wasn't in the walk-in cupboard or the walnut wardrobe.

By now the girls were shouting his name, enjoying the fact that we couldn't find him. We had a quick but thorough look in mine and Sally's bedroom, but he wasn't in there either, so he had to be upstairs again. The top floor held my office, another bathroom and the spare bedroom. As soon as we'd looked in all three I began seriously to wonder where he might be. It occurred to me that, although I couldn't imagine how he might have done it, there was the tiniest of possibilities that he could have slipped past us while we were in his room and nipped downstairs. So I ran downstairs and re-checked every possible hiding place. It didn't take long;

I knew where they all were by now. I made my way back upstairs like a cop with a search warrant, clearing rooms as I went, mentally chalking a cross on the door, one stroke on the way in, another as I left. Back at the top of the house, I finally admitted to myself that I was anxious.

Harry was good at hide and seek, but not this good. How was it possible, in a house I knew so well, for him to vanish so completely? I forced myself to be calm and to stick to a methodological approach. He couldn't have left the house—the front and back doors were locked, as were the windows. The door to the cellar was kept bolted. The door leading to the crawlspace that was all that was left of the loft after its conversion was not locked, but it was inaccessible behind the ratty old settee in my office and neither of our children had ever shown the slightest interest in it. I looked down at Sophie and Agnes. Their eyes were wide with excitement. Sophie was jumping up and down, shouting Harry's name.

Follow me, I said, something having made me think of triple-checking his favourite hiding place. In Harry's bedroom I got down on all fours and pulled out the plastic toy crate from under his bed. There he was, in the far corner, still as a statue, scarcely breathing. His eyes met mine and he started to smile.

He crawled out and I hugged him so tightly he protested that it hurt.

I'd lost my appetite for hide and seek, but naturally the kids hadn't and Sophie was insisting on hiding next. I knew if I stopped the game there'd be trouble, so we counted to twenty while she toddled off. It took us less than another twenty seconds to find her, a tell-tale giggling lump under the duvet in mine and Sally's bed.

In fairness, I now had to let Agnes go off and hide, despite overwhelming tiredness on my part and a growing desire to head back downstairs, open a beer and listen to the news on the radio while allowing the kids to veg out in front of Cartoon Network. I couldn't expect either William or Sally for another fifteen minutes.

. . . eighteen, nineteen, *twenty*!

The first place Harry looked was under his own bed. I think we might have heard if she'd hidden in here, I suggested, but in fact we hadn't heard anything at all. She'd managed to slip out and hide without leaving us any clues.

Let's look in Mummy and Daddy's room, Harry urged.

Sophie instantly copied what he'd said in her more condensed delivery, in which all the words ran together and could only be decoded by remembering what had been said before.

Agnes wasn't in Mummy and Daddy's room. The three of us climbed the stairs again to the top floor. Spare bedroom, bathroom, my office—all clear. Back down to the first floor. Bathroom, Sophie's room—both empty. We trooped downstairs, Harry running on ahead, wanting to be the one to find Agnes. There was no sign of her in the lounge, dining room or kitchen. Back in the hall, I noticed her shoes at the bottom of the stairs. She'd taken them off just after coming into the house.

I checked the locks on the doors and windows, then we ran back up to the first floor. I looked under each of the beds, behind all the curtains, in every cupboard. I added my voice to those of Harry and Sophie. I shouted that her dad was due to collect her and he'd want to get straight back. It was time to come out. She'd won. (*No, I won!* Harry protested.) Come on, come on out, Agnes!

I ran up to the top floor without waiting for Harry and Sophie. I shoved the settee in the office out of the way and yanked open the door to the crawlspace, shining a light inside. Fishing tackle, rolled-up film posters, Christmas decorations, stacks of used padded envelopes, suitcases full of old clothes I couldn't bear to throw away—but no little girl, no Agnes. I looked under my desk, behind the oversize books on the bottom shelves of the bookcases, in the corner between the radio and the radiator. Running back out of my office I collided with Sophie on her way in. She fell over and started crying, but I ran on, into the spare bedroom. I ripped the sheets off the bed, hauled the TV away from the wall. In the adjoining bathroom I tore aside the shower curtain.

As I took the stairs three at a time back down to the next floor I could hear that both children were crying now. In our bedroom I emptied the laundry basket, fought my way through the dresses in Sally's wardrobe. I made myself stop and stare into the room's reflection in the full-length mirror in case that revealed any hidden detail I had somehow otherwise missed. I ran into Sophie's room and climbed up on to a chair to open the door to the linen cupboard.

I had checked everywhere, every possible hiding place, and she wasn't to be found. She'd gone.

The door bell rang. Sophie's room was just at the top of the stairs, so I could see right down to the front door. Through the frosted glass I could see that it wasn't Sally. Anyway, she would have used her keys. It was William.

The Blink

I'm having a drink with Gina Hamilton in a hotel bar in Manchester.

"This place has changed," she says.

"You haven't," I say. "You look as gorgeous as ever."

When she smiles she reveals her front teeth, one of which leans slightly back and the other slightly forward.

"I hope you don't mind me coming to see you," she says.

I refill her glass. "I can honestly say I've never minded you coming to see me."

She smiles, then looks away; the smile vanishes.

"I had to get out of London," she says. "I couldn't go out. Wherever I went, they were after me."

I look into my wine glass. "You have to admit, it was pretty funny."

"I can't understand why nobody saw it," she says.

"Plenty of people have seen it. It went viral."

"I mean before it went out. You know what I mean. The editor, the director. God, even the bloody critics."

"Maybe one of them did. Imagine you're a TV critic and you see that. What would you do? Email the programme makers in the vain hope they can fix it before it goes out or write it up and hope it stays in? It's good copy."

Gina had always wanted to be an actress—and I do mean actress. This was when not only were you *allowed* to use the word, but it was the word you were *supposed* to use. If you were a girl—and I do mean girl—and you said you wanted to be an actor, people would have, as Gina once put it, looked at you funny. Hers was the first hand to go up at school when volunteers were sought for the end-of-year production. At university she was so busy at Dramsoc she narrowly avoided being kicked off her course for poor attendance. I was studying journalism, Gina English, so we wouldn't even have met had we not been in the same hall. I used to leave my door open and I'd see her walking past, nose in a book. I asked what was so good that she couldn't put it down. It was a play script, covered in highlighter. I said I'd go and see it if she let me know when and where. She did and here we are, thirty years later.

If, in the past couple of decades, I've seen more of Gina on TV than in the flesh, that's mostly a reflection of how her career took off. If she was filming in the north she would let me know—sometimes—and we would have a drink and a catch-up. When my on-off relationship with a Chorlton psychotherapist was off—and sometimes, if I'm honest, when I wasn't sure if it was on or off—Gina and I might allow the evening to be extended into the night.

"It's also good publicity," I say, upending the bottle over Gina's glass. "Shall I get us another? I'll get another."

I go to the bar. As I'm waiting I fiddle with a pack of breath mints and watch someone enter the bar. I'm not sure if it's a man or a woman. My attention is drawn to the figure's awkward progress towards the bar. I'm going to go with female, even while no doubt breaking a dozen social codes by wanting to nail down gender. She moves like she's already drunk—I'll be surprised if they serve her—or has had to learn to walk again after a stroke. There's a deliberateness about the placing of her feet. Even the swing of her arms looks practised.

"That's just twenty-nine pounds, sir."

I turn back to the bar and look at the young man behind it placing an opened bottle of white wine on the counter.

"Just?" I say and pop a mint into my mouth.

"You ordered the Sauvignon, sir. The house is only nineteen."

"Only?"

He looks at me blankly.

"Contactless?" I say.

I take the bottle of wine back to our table and notice that Gina is looking at the new arrival with an expression approaching alarm.

"Shit," she says.

The thing was that Gina *was* making fewer appearances on TV whether I realised it or not. The offers weren't drying up but the gaps between parts were getting longer. I blame the effects of the ageing process on me for my not realising this, time seeming to pass more quickly, meaning that I telescoped six months into as many weeks, and the reason for the lengthening gaps should have been obvious to me.

Apparently I'm unusual in finding middle-aged women more interesting to look at and, yes, more attractive. Most people—most men?—prefer to look at younger women in films and TV dramas where the part is a middle-aged woman, or should be. So either the part is written for a younger woman or it's written for a middle-aged woman and a younger woman is found to play it. Either way, it gets harder for middle-aged "female actors" to find parts, so, hoping for regular work, maybe Gina and other actresses started going for parts they might not otherwise have gone for.

The Academy of Motion Picture Arts and Sciences still gives awards to the Best Actress in a Leading Role and the Best Actress in a Supporting Role, but for how much longer? What about Princess Grace of Monaco, who won an Oscar in 1955? Must we call her Prince Grace of Monaco? What about Princess Diana? Princess Anne? The rap artist known as Actress, and Princess Michael of Kent?

I'm pouring her a glass of wine, but Gina has an elbow on the table and a hand in front of her face.

"She's seen me," she says. "I know she has."

"Who has?"

"Woman at the bar who's just come in. She's one of them."

"That's what we used to say, isn't it, 'one of them', or what our parents used to say? What do we say now? LGBT."

"LGBTQ," she says with a half-smile.

"LGBTQQ," I say.

Gina looks at me from under her shielding hand. "LGBTQQI."

"Hmm." I narrow my eyes and purse my lips. "LGBTQQIS."

"S?"

"Straight. Apparently. So my friend Tony told me yesterday."

"Is your friend Tony slightly homophobic?"

"Well, he was sitting next to his husband when he told me, so I doubt it."

"Oh God, look, she's on her mobile." Gina is looking over my shoulder.

"So?"

"She'll be rounding up all her mates." Gina knocks back the rest of her wine.

"That's thirty quid a bottle," I say.

It did go viral, but let me remind you. Gina had a part in a crime drama. ITV, post watershed, I forget the name of it, but aren't they all essentially the same, especially on ITV? The body of a woman is found, usually a young woman, as discussed. Crime scene tape. Flashing blue lights. SoCos in white suits. A white tent. SIO, distinctive in some way—

we'll get to know her in a short scene at home later. Bluff pathologist—seen it all. Rookie policewoman, maybe.

Gina turns up half an hour in. She's a witness. Her character is barely sketched in—good job, nice husband, couple of kids—and then she's killed in an RTA that is probably not an accident. She's on the slab in the morgue, just lying there while the SIO and the pathologist exchange a few lines of dialogue across her legs. She's covered up, for modesty, but her face is exposed and she blinks.

How come, as Gina says, no one saw it? No one on set, no one looking at the rushes. The editor doesn't see it later. The director doesn't see it. No one sees it who is connected with the production. Unbelievable.

Yet thousands of viewers see it. Social media goes crazy. People take the piss, because it's funny. But then it gets serious, when the aggrieved voices make themselves heard and their owners start mobilising, and it's not so funny any more and Gina gets out of town.

Gina's hands grip the sides of the table and she starts to lever herself up, but then I'm aware of movement behind me. The woman from the bar draws level.

"Excuse me," she says in a harsh, cracked voice.

Gina sits back down, her features flat with resignation.

"Do you mind if I ask," the woman says, "are you Gina Hamilton?" The skin of her face, lit by the candle on our table, is papery. There's the faint scent of Listerine on the air that briefly masks an underlying smell of soap, formaldehyde and the flowers of those invasive Himalayan plants that grow by the river.

Gina looks up, raises her eyebrows.

"Would you like to sit down?" I ask the woman, who ignores me. They don't so much like sitting down; standing, walking and lying down are more their thing. Lying down

I get. I'm not so sure about the standing and walking, and wonder if it might not be a bit of PR. Gina looks at me.

I'm aware of shapes passing by outside the windows, then a group appears at the entrance to the bar, their white faces turning this way and that like searchlights. One of them points in our direction and they start to move across the room, bumping into tables, causing eye-rolls and tuts among drinkers. It's like the remake of *Night of the Living Dead* that Mike Leigh always promised he wouldn't do.

Their first campaign revolved around extras. Bodies on battlefields or at crime scenes. Corpses in the morgue, toes with labels sticking out of sheets, having assumed no previous active role in the drama. Only dead actors should play these parts, they said, and their campaign, aggressively mounted, quickly gained momentum. A live actor playing such a part very soon became the equivalent of a white actor blacking up.

Until Gina's blink, a live actor playing a live part who then dies and, crucially, enjoys a certain amount of screen time dead had been a grey area. Dead actors argued they should play the part, either in a switch at the point of death, which would require body-doubling or lots of expensive make-up, or right from the start. Live actors maintained that that was ridiculous: the dead couldn't convincingly play the living, while the living could easily handle lying still.

The blink changed all that.

"It's our *Philadelphia*," said the dead, referring to Tom Hanks's portrayal of gay lawyer with AIDS Andrew Beckett, a part that, it was argued by some, should have been played by a gay actor.

Good luck finding an openly gay actor in Hollywood in 1993.

❀

"Do you think it was right?" the woman asks Gina. "Do you think you were the right actor for that role? I don't think so. *We* don't think so." Having been leaning forward to deliver her rebuke to Gina, she now straightens up at the waist and takes a half-step back as if to become one with the mob that has gathered around her.

For all the potency of George Romero's images of shambling hordes, they were, as we now know, a guess. The dead are not especially sociable. They don't hang out together and the living tend not to encounter them in groups. The effect of being this close to a large group of them now begins to show on Gina's face, which wears an expression of mild disgust. She gets to her feet and moves sideways around the table, so that it forms a barrier between her and them. Feeling at a strange disadvantage remaining seated, I also get up, but from the wrong side of my chair, so that I end up standing with the group looking across the table at Gina. She looks at me, it seems to me, accusingly. I suck on the last of my mint and feel myself shrugging back at her.

The Empty Flat

One weekend in the summer two people appear in the flat directly across the courtyard from mine. A well-built middle-aged white woman with shoulder-length hair held back from her face with an Alice band, and a younger woman, also white, slighter in build, blonde, topknot. The flat has been empty for weeks, months even. Two, three months.

The two women spend the morning cleaning the kitchen, working together for an hour or so, then the older woman moves into the bathroom, to the left of the kitchen. It has frosted glass, but there's frosted glass and frosted glass. She moves around in there cleaning with apparent vigour. They work together again in the bedroom, which is to the left of the bathroom. They spend the day cleaning, occasionally disappearing into the front bedroom and the living room, only part of which can be seen through the kitchen window, provided the interconnecting door has been left open.

The courtyard is approximately forty yards across. It's possible to read the brand on a cereal packet in the kitchen of the flat, with a reasonable pair of binoculars.

By the middle of the evening, dusk having begun to settle and no lights having come on in the flat, I realise they have finished for the day and gone out—or left. They do not return, either that night or on the Sunday morning.

During the week, they do not return. On the following Saturday morning I am at my kitchen window, a student's work untouched on the kitchen table behind me, but they do not reappear. Nor during the week that follows. Nor the next weekend and so on and so forth. They had *not* been moving in, a single mother and her daughter, perhaps, or an advance party for a larger family group, husband-father held up or otherwise occupied. They had been cleaning the flat for the letting agents. Although they hadn't particularly *looked* like cleaners, that was what they were. Either professional cleaners or, it now occurs to me, possibly the owner of the flat and her daughter.

A plastic bottle of cleaning fluid, left by the two women, stands on the kitchen window ledge. It is not a brand I have used.

The empty flat remains empty. Life goes on in the flat to the left—the early middle-aged Asian couple—and the flat to the right—the young white couple in their twenties, and in the flats below—the tall, grey-haired man, a cycling enthusiast who lives alone and every Saturday morning dresses in Lycra and carries his bike down the open back stairs. The two hipster-bearded men in their thirties distinguishible by body shape and degree of conviviality when they entertain, which is most Friday nights. The single black woman in one of the ground-floor flats who smokes on the open landing outside her kitchen door despite living alone. The Japanese couple in the flat next door to hers, their kitchen windows semi-permanently steamed up.

The empty flat remains empty.

The sun starts to set noticeably earlier in the evening, above the flats opposite. The work piles up on the kitchen table behind me.

Still the windows of the empty flat remain dark.

I open my notebook and write a list:

Prostate cancer
Bowel cancer
Brain tumour
Lymphoma/leukaemia
Stomach cancer
Stroke
Heart disease
Accident
Random attack
Dementia

Term will soon be starting and at various points during the week I travel into town and sit at my desk in a large shared office. I stare at my laptop, but all I can see on-screen are the reflections of the overhead fluorescent lights. I have tried, on previous occasions, sitting at other people's desks, but there is nowhere in the office where the reflections are not an issue. I look up and across the office at a colleague who is sitting at her desk, typing on her desktop computer. She has her back to me. I know who she is. We have shared an office, with several other people, for almost a year and prior to that, when we were in the old building, I would see her once or twice a week. Twice a term I would sit in a departmental meeting with her and many others for up to three hours. I have known her for the ten years that I have been working here, but I can't remember her name.

I know who she is, what she looks like from the front—even though I am now looking at her back—and what she does, what she teaches, what her research interests are, who she likes and doesn't like, even who likes her and doesn't like her, but I can't think of her name. The more intently I reach for it, the further it retreats from my grasp. I used to know it. I've known it all the time I've known her and who she is. I still know who she is, but I've forgotten her name.

I could find it out. I could squint past the reflections on my screen and open the web page devoted to the names and research interests and contact details of my colleagues, but I don't. I should be able to remember it.

I close my laptop, slip it into my bag and leave the office.

On the way home I read an article in the paper about how loneliness is becoming a bigger killer than either cancer or heart disease.

The bottle of cleaning fluid still stands on the window ledge of the empty flat. In the evening no lights are turned on. Neither in the kitchen of the empty flat, nor in my kitchen as long as I'm standing at the window.

I open my notebook and cross out number nine, "Random attack", and write in "Loneliness".

Although teaching doesn't start until next week, work is busy, a lot of staff and students coming and going. I am standing in the lobby talking to my colleague, Joe, when a young woman appears. I know who she is. I can remember how we became friends, when her father, a British man of Nigerian origin who looks after a number of student houses, rescued my laptop from an opportunist thief and handed it in to the police after it fell off the back of my bike, when I still cycled to work. When he told me his daughter was interested in my field I offered to mentor her. I have read her work, I have even spent two separate weeks in her company on residential courses. I know where she lives, what she wants to do and even vaguely recall mention of her getting some work at our place, which is presumably what she is doing here now, but I can't remember her name.

I say hello to her and ask her if she knows Joe and then, mid-introduction, I reach for my phone in my pocket and ask to be excused as I've been waiting for a call. By the time I return to them, they have performed their own introductions.

In my kitchen, I open my notebook and turn to my list. I take what was number ten, "Dementia", and put it at number two, switching with "Bowel cancer". Then I move "Dementia" to number one and put "Prostate cancer" at number two.

By the weekend, three people have appeared in the empty flat. Two women and a man. The women are not the same women who had cleaned the flat in the summer. All three are white and in their forties. He is stocky, powerful looking but slow, almost ponderous in his movements. The two women move around him relatively nimbly, although they, too, are heavily built. They have dark hair, shoulder length; one wears a striped top, the other a fleece. The three appear to know each other but other than that it is impossible to say with any certainty what their relationships are to each other. There are only two bedrooms in the flat, however.

On the Saturday night they cook a meal and eat, out of sight, in the living room, where a line of cards can be seen standing on the front window ledge. Birthday cards? Good luck in your new home cards? In the kitchen, the plastic bottle of cleaning fluid has been moved, or thrown out, and some new objects have taken up residence. A green plastic chopping board. A red bowl.

When they clean up later, all three of them work together again. The man washes, one of the women dries and the other woman bobs around putting things away. That woman—the woman in the striped top—keeps going out of the back door to the store cupboard on the balcony by the back stairs. Some of the things that need to be put away she puts away in the store cupboard. When he has finished washing up, the man goes outside also for a smoke.

On Sunday there is no sign of activity. Either they went out early or are sleeping late.

On my list in my notebook I switch "Loneliness" and "Brain tumour".

By Sunday night, were it not for the green plastic chopping board and red bowl, the flat opposite would appear to be the empty flat again.

At work we have a department away day. We don't go far, just to the library of a very old school in town. I take my place next to Joe, then turn to see a new colleague enter the room. I know who she is. I sat on the interview panel that gave her her job. Prior to that I had worked with her when she had been a visiting speaker. I have known her for years, perhaps eight years. She is a British woman of Pakistani heritage, a scriptwriter and poet and former policewoman. She is extremely gregarious, a lively presence on a work night out. But I can't remember her name.

That evening, the empty flat is in darkness. I wait until quite late and then unlock my back door and walk down the back stairs to the courtyard. I cross the courtyard and start climbing the steps to the top flats on the far side. At the top I turn left and approach the back door to the flat opposite mine. I look at the door handle, recalling as I do so the frequency with which the new residents had gone in and out. I see my hand reaching out to take hold of it.

The Dummy

The featureless road. The driving rain.

White lines, empty fields.

The endless rhythm of the stop-go shunt, a Newton's cradle of cars on the motorway heading north-west. The occasional church spire in the distance piercing the dark grey wadding of the clouds. The monotony is relieved by a fizzing spot of fluorescent yellow up ahead. You squint, peer through the windscreen, rub with your sleeve at a stubborn patch of fog on the glass. The view clears. The fluorescent spot grows, elongates, becomes a figure.

The motorway narrows from three lanes down to two. The traffic slows accordingly. The man in the high-visibility clothing moves his left arm up and down, telling you to slow down further. He's standing hard by the crash barrier on the central reservation. He's either suicidal or insane or both. There has to be a better way to warn drivers of impending hazards, you think. Sure, he's completely covered in hi-vis gear, from the hood of his jacket to the turn-ups of his trousers, but you can't imagine this man's UK counterpart happily standing that close to moving traffic in the fast lane of the M1. Maybe the Belgians pay danger money, or perhaps, as seems likely from the standard of the driving, all Belgians are clinically insane. Admittedly this may be the birthplace of surrealism, but still.

You twist your head for a closer look as you roll past. The planes of his face seem abnormally severe, his skin unnaturally smooth. Do motorway maintenance workers really shave every morning?

"Tell me where it comes from, this love of our country."

Asking the question was a striking young woman of slender build and average height, her irregularly cut mahogany-coloured hair framing a face shaped like a warning sign. Eyes that glittered; a short, sharp nose, pointed like the bill of a goldfinch; lips painted a vivid red. When she leaned forward across the hotel breakfast table, peripheral vision gifted me a view down the front of her top.

"What's not to love about it?" I said, careful not to let my eyes drop. "Beer, chocolate, medieval architecture."

"In that order?"

She flashed her teeth; one was chipped at the corner. Either her lower lip was uneven or she twisted it unconsciously while she spoke. I remembered reading somewhere that beauty was all down to symmetry. I'd thought it was rubbish at the time and now here was proof.

"Definitely."

"No, but . . . " she started, signalling the switch to serious interview mode by picking up a sachet of sugar and turning it end on end on the tablecloth. "The Eddy De Groot novels are bestsellers. You're not telling me his creator is inspired by nothing more than a desire to sit drinking Duvel at pavement cafés in the Grote Markt?"

"With a view of the Stadhuis."

"Exactly."

"No. In fact, just between you and me," I said, lowering my voice to a conspiratorial whisper, "I don't actually like Duvel."

She sat back, eyes wide.

"I know, I know," I said, hands in the air. "The man who didn't like Duvel. I don't like tripels either. I like blonde beers. I've always been partial to blondes." I gave her my winning grin.

"Only blondes?" she asked, sitting forward again.

"As you probably know if you've read the books, I like the brown beers best." My eyes flicked down momentarily. "Westmalle, Ename, Chimay—but only the red or the blue."

Around us, hotel staff were discreetly clearing tables.

"So, Eddy De Groot, your Flemish detective, is you?" she asked, bending the sugar sachet in half.

"It's easier than making stuff up."

"Your alter ego?"

"If you like. All I know is he's not Poirot and he's not Maigret, but he's not Van der Valk either. I saw a gap in the market for a Dutch-speaking Belgian detective. Written by an Englishman."

Now it was my turn to sit back in my chair. I took my eyes off her for a moment and looked around the breakfast room. She had described my Eddy De Groot novels as bestsellers. Which of course they weren't, not in the UK, but they did okay in Dutch translation. In addition, they probably sold as many English copies here in Belgium and in Holland as they did back home, there were that many English speakers in the Low Countries. In any case, the figures obviously added up, or I wouldn't get this treatment: five-star hotel, a reading slot at the Antwerp festival, a round of interviews with local and national media. The girl with the sexy mouth had come up from Brussels to do a piece for *De Standaard*. I wasn't kidding myself it was going to last for ever, but I might as well enjoy it while I could.

"It goes back to when I was a kid," I said, leaning forward and taking the sachet of sugar from her hand. "My dad used to bring me stamps off the ships. He was a customs officer and he used to rummage ships in the docks and bring me back stamps for my collection. The ones I liked best were the Belgian stamps. The picture of King Baudouin, the different colours. Pink, blue, green. Brown and grey. I liked the way the colours changed but the image remained the same. I wanted to own the whole set. I like having whole sets of things. Belgian stamps. Agatha Christie novels—Fontana paperbacks with the Tom Adams covers. No others." I toyed with the sugar sachet and shrugged my shoulders. "It's a man thing."

I watched her check the digital voice recorder.

"When's your deadline?" I asked. "Do you have to go away and write this up this morning?"

"I've got till tomorrow lunchtime," she said.

"So what do you say we do this over lunch?"

I held my breath and caught her looking at my wedding ring. I said nothing. She smiled.

Rain falls without end from a sky made of lead. Your eyes are gritty. Your head lolls momentarily over the wheel.

Microsleep.

You exit the motorway. Pull over, rub your face. Get out, walk up and down. Fresh air, pouring rain. Get back in the car. Sit there looking out at the rain. You get your phone out of your pocket and stare at it. You check that you haven't missed any calls or texts. You haven't. You remember the time you spent ten minutes going all over the house looking for the phone, while talking on what you thought was the cordless landline. You even told the person you were talking to that you were looking for your mobile, and all the while you were holding it in your hand and talking on it.

This wasn't so long ago.

You told your wife about it, hoping she would find it funny. She shook her head and said, "It's a bit early even for you, isn't it?" You had had a drink, as it happened, but nothing more than that. You wondered if she had a point and you decided that she may well have done, but that it was disappointing all the same that she didn't just laugh about it and then perhaps everything would have been all right.

It's a long time since everything has been all right.

You go to the messages on your phone and reread the last text she sent. There's no real need, there are no fresh insights to be gained. You're just tormenting yourself.

You put the phone back into your pocket and turn the key in the ignition.

More rain, more flat fields. Grey streets with occasional brick houses, shuttered, stark. More traffic cones, roadworks, another flash of fluorescent yellow. But the perspective's all wrong. It looks like he's lying down. You lean forward over the wheel, screwing up your eyes. He *is* lying down. Pull over, stop. Get out. Jacket over your head. Bend down. His hood over his face. Limbs at weird angles, as if he's been knocked down. Hit and run. You pull the hood back a little.

The face isn't real. The rain doesn't roll off it in quite the right way. But the arms and legs look right; the torso is reassuringly bulky. You touch the leg. It's a real leg. You'd put money on it being a real leg. You haven't had a drink yet today. You squeeze harder. Maybe you're wrong. You look at the face again. Is it a mask? You remember the man on the tube, the blind man with the rubber eye mask. Two unblinking eyes painted on to a rubber mask held in place with elastic behind a pair of useless glasses. When you sat opposite, you stared at him so hard you ended up having to look away, because you became convinced he could see you doing it. Somehow.

When you took a photograph of him through a crowd on the platform and showed it to your wife, she called you a sick fuck, but only after making sure the children were not in the room.

You took your camera with you when you went to say goodnight to the children, because you wanted to show that picture to them. You thought they'd get it. But they were both already asleep, their hands clenched into tiny fists, mouths slightly open. The infinitesimal rise and fall of the chest. You bent right down over their beds until you could feel their breath on your cheek. The faintly sour smell. You would never stop loving them, you told yourself, no matter what they did. Yes, you'd lose your temper with them and yell at them, and afterwards you would feel bad because the anger melted away leaving only the love behind.

You couldn't imagine life without them.

Sometimes you'd sit and watch them breathe, sitting with one and then the other. Until your wife would call you. I thought you'd gone to the pub, she would say when you went downstairs. No, you'd say, and you'd look into her eyes and see if it was still there, the glimmer in her eyes that had drawn you to her, what, twelve years ago? Thirteen? It had lost some of its candlepower, perhaps, but it was still there, and so you'd hold her and you'd hug each other tightly and you'd say you loved her and you hoped she'd be patient with you and she'd say nothing, but nor would she let go of you.

You try to loosen the collar on the shirt, just in case. The neck looks no more realistic than the face close up. You look up, look around. There's no one. The nearest buildings are some distance away. There's no traffic. You gather the dummy's legs and thread your arm under his back, taking care to support the head with your upper arm. He's lighter than a fully grown man. Heavier than either of your children. You carry him the few yards back to the car and manage to open the passenger door. Your heart is beating fast and the blood vessels in your head are throbbing. You position his legs in the footwell and once you've got the seatbelt around him he sits up okay. His head hangs forward just a little.

You check your mirrors. There's a car in the wing mirror, far enough away for its driver not to have seen anything. In any case, your car would have acted as a shield. The other car now drives past without slowing down. You wait for the ringing in your head, from the hiss of the tyres on the wet road surface, to die down and then you pull out and drive on.

I took her to the Entrepôt du Congo for lunch and between us we got through so many Rodenbachs neither of us thought it was a bad idea when I suggested we carry on the interview back at my hotel. Of course when we got back there, the lobby area was busy and returning to the breakfast room didn't feel like an attractive option, so although I know I could have asked the concierge for conference facilities, it just seemed easier to head upstairs to my room.

We did finish the interview, but let's just say it took a while to get started on the afternoon session. Hilde said it was the first interview she'd conducted in which both parties were completely naked.

"Both parties?" I said.

She smiled.

We could have perhaps left it at that and not gone on and ruined everything. But during the time we spent in my room there were moments of tenderness, interludes when we lay side by side catching our breath gazing into each other's eyes like lovers. Most of the time, admittedly, it felt like a one-night stand, but there were moments when it didn't. And there was a mutual reluctance to part once we were dressed and Hilde said the batteries on her digital recorder were exhausted but that it didn't matter because she'd already got far more material than she could use. Somehow we ended up at a bar not far from the hotel drinking shots. I switched my phone back on to see that my wife had been trying to get hold of me. Instead of calling her back I ordered another round of drinks and heard myself answering Hilde's question about the origins of my love of Belgium in greater depth.

"It wasn't just the stamps," I said. "Well, it was, but it wasn't just the stamps per se. It was what they symbolised. They were like the equivalent British stamps. Different colours, monarch's head. We had a queen, you had a king. I couldn't get my head around how strange it must be to have a king rather than a queen." I knocked back another shot and was about to order more, but checked myself and ordered two dark beers instead. "We should drink them slowly," I said. "Here was this country," I went on, "just across the Channel from us. A small country, a monarchy. In a way it was a mirror image of Britain. As I grew up, I imagined that it was like a parallel world to the one in which I lived."

Red light struck one side of her face, blue the other. I felt a compulsion to open up to her completely, to tell her everything about myself. In turn, I wanted to know everything there was to know about her. I took out my wallet and withdrew the battered picture of my kids that went everywhere with me.

"Jack and May," I said.

She grinned and tossed her hair back and asked me how old they were. I told her eight and six, but that the photograph was a year old. She handed it back and as I slipped it into my wallet I fell into a sort of fugue. I couldn't work out why. Eventually I wondered if it was because she'd been happy to see a picture of my children. If she was happy that I had kids, did that mean she would also be happy when I went home to them, which I both did and didn't want to do.

✻

You went home, of course. But it was clear—not to them, but to your wife—that something was up. You can't dissemble, can't hide the truth. You said nothing, but within a week you were back in Belgium. Another book to research, you said, next in the series. You stayed with Hilde. She was single even if you weren't.

You scrapped a planned De Groot novel and started a new one. He'd fallen in love, with a journalist. His job was on the line, his life falling apart. De Groot's wife was suspicious; yours was too. It wasn't as if she read your work-in-progress, not normally, but accessing your back-ups remotely on your iDisk was beyond neither her imagination nor her technical know-how. Getting the password right was the easy part, since you had never had any secrets. The drink and drug habits had never been kept from her. How could they be? Their effects were written all over your face and bank statements.

When you got home, your wife confronted you and you broke down and confessed. You sat at the kitchen table and looked out of the window while she threw crockery—wedding presents—at the wall. In the garden, perched on the handrail that runs around the outside of the deck area, was a small green bird, a greenfinch, seemingly completely oblivious to the mayhem taking place only a few feet away. You watched that bird, its tiny head shifting position in jerky increments, and were filled with a vague longing. If you could have put your feelings into words you would perhaps have said that you wanted to swap places with the bird. That you wanted your spirit or your soul to escape from your own body like smoke and drift under the kitchen door and then enter the greenfinch, which you would henceforth, in some strange incomprehensible way, become.

Do you even believe in a spirit or a soul? Or is there nothing but a mind? A consciousness? A sense of identity?

You see a sign for Westvleteren and leave the main road. Some say Westvleteren 12 is the best beer in the world and you would not disagree. None of the three Westvleteren beers can be bought anywhere other than direct from the Westvleteren Abbey brewery. You've heard they even require you to have an appointment, but if you turn up and say give me an appointment in five minutes' time, what are they going to do? Turn you away? Or sell you some of the best beer in the world?

You see his yellow jacket out of the corner of your eye and it startles you. You'd forgotten he was there, sitting right next to you, steam rising off him. His raised hood conceals his profile. Didn't you lower his hood? You must have raised it again, either deliberately or accidentally, while getting him into the car.

You keep driving, although the signs to Westvleteren have disappeared. There was a village, or a hamlet. A settlement. Three or four buildings, all shuttered, no gardens. Brick fronts hard by the road. But no crossroads, no turnings, unless you missed one while sneaking a look at your passenger. Here's something on the left. You slow down. A walled enclosure. Carefully cut grass. Regular lines of white headstones. Identical black lettering on each.

You accelerate slowly as if out of respect. There is no let-up in the rain. At the next turning you go left. The windscreen wipers sound like a heartbeat. A Coca-Cola sign shimmers out of the gloom on the right-hand side of the road. You pull over and stop. Some kind of café. Step out of the car and lock it, then look back in and hesitate, the rain drumming on your shoulders and the back of your neck, before unlocking it and turning to walk towards the café.

I took the Eurostar back to Brussels and jumped in a cab. We spent the afternoon in Hilde's flat on avenue Emile

Max. When I finally looked out of the window I saw a flash of green as a bird the size of a jackdaw, but much more streamlined with pointed wings and a long tail, swooped down into the garden and then climbed back up from its dive just as quickly, like a BMXer on a ramp. I knew instantly what bird it was.

"Look," I said to Hilde, "a ringed-neck parakeet. They've become common in London, apparently, though I've never seen one. I had to come to Brussels to see my first one. It's an omen."

She asked me what had happened in London.

"She told me to fuck off," I said. And straight away, as a shadow seemed to pass across her face, I knew it was a strategic error. You don't tell your lover that your wife has kicked you out. It doesn't matter that you may have talked about the possibility. When it happens, you say nothing, unless what you want to end up with is precisely that, nothing.

We went out to a bar in Schaerbeek where a friend of Hilde's was celebrating a birthday. I drank steadily as I watched Hilde drinking and sitting with her arms around a succession of people, male and female, all of them younger than me, as she was herself of course, and I started to feel obscurely sad. Self-pity pricked at my eyes as I turned to look out of the window and thought about Jack and May.

And Sara. My wife.

I left the bar and walked in a random direction. Before long I realised I had entered the red light district by the Gare du Nord and I went into the next bar I came to. Pinewood panelling covered the walls. I ordered an Orval because it appeared to be the only beer they had. I detest Orval, so I drank it quickly and ordered another. And then another. It was dark when I left the bar. Red, blue and ultraviolet lights slid past me in a sickening blur. When I somehow found my way back to avenue Emile Max, I waited outside

Hilde's building until someone came out. The door to her flat gave easily enough without causing too much damage, but really I was past caring. While I was blundering around inside looking for her car keys, I felt my phone vibrating in my pocket. A text message.

You don't like Jupiler any more than Orval, but when it's all they've got, you'll swallow it. Three small bottles. Take the edge off. A fat man sits at a till. You give him a handful of coins and go on through into a long narrow room filled with dusty display cases containing scraps of battle dress, a scabbard, a German helmet. Strange wooden boxes squat on tables. You put your eye to the eyepiece and twist the knob to change the photograph being viewed. Some optical trickery inside the box creates a 3D effect. Pictures of terrible wounds and corpses alternate with photographs of advancing columns of soldiers. The atrocity exhibition with slot machines. Somehow, their being in black and white makes it worse, but after a while, the pictures no longer shock. You become inured to the horror. At the far end of the room a doorway leads outside.

You follow a path into a field dotted with trees and lined, you now see, with passageways dug into the earth.

Trenches.

You remember the cemetery filled with war dead. Are these real trenches or some sick replica, a theme park, dug by the fat man? Or that the fat man had dug for him? From what you know of Belgium, it would not surprise you at all to learn that these are the real thing. In another country this would be a monument. Here it's a disgrace. You'd almost rather it were the fat man's plaything, that just one man was to blame instead of a federal state for failing to honour the sacrifice of others.

You half-clamber, half-slip down into one of the trenches and it's all you can do to remain on your feet in the mud.

You feel a damp sensation on the left side of your chest. Something trickling. Sweat from all the exertion. You feel like a ghoul. Time to leave.

You collapse in the driver's seat. Turn to look at your passenger.

"Weird place," you say, and wait for a response. "Suit yourself. Let's go."

You realise you've not taken your coat off and Hilde's car will now be covered in mud.

"Too bad," you say. "She should have thought of that." And you laugh.

You know you shouldn't be driving, but you don't care. You can feel that wet sensation on the left side of your chest again. Still sweating? You look down, tugging at your coat. There's blood. Quite a lot of blood. Stop the car. Pull at your t-shirt, covered in blood.

There's a big hole in your chest. Fist-sized. As if something has been torn out of you.

You bend over to look more closely. Tentatively insert the tips of your fingers. Your hand slowly falls away and you look up through the windscreen at the ever-falling rain. The only sound you can hear, apart from the rattling of the rain, to which you have become so accustomed you don't notice it any more, is the *ba-dum ba-dum ba-dum* of the wipers.

The text said she had taken the kids and gone. I could come back, she said, but they wouldn't be there. I'd be coming back to an empty house.

It wasn't like she was kidnapping them and I'd never see them again. They'd be going to school as normal and I could hang around the school gate. But I wouldn't get to be with them properly. I could fight it, but I knew I didn't have a hope.

It was a long text.

I got in Hilde's car and drove out of Brussels, heading north-west towards the coast. Not that I had any kind of plan. It was already late and dark, and the combination of alcohol, tiredness and the constant rain meant I had to stop. I found a DIY superstore with a large car park on the outskirts of Ghent. I parked by the wall facing the exit and slept on the back seat. In the morning I went in search of food, then sat in the car while waiting for the DIY store to open. I went in, got what I wanted and returned to the car with it coiled in a plastic bag, which I put in the boot. I then drove on with no fixed destination in mind.

There was a pain in my chest. From having slept badly, I presumed.

You drive until you reach the coast. Still it rains. The first cheap hotel you see, you leave the car and carry the dummy in over your shoulder. The woman gives you a twin room. You lay him on one of the beds and you take the other, kicking off your shoes. You turn and turn but sleep won't come. You get up and gently move him along a little so that you can get on the same bed. Facing away from him. You lie absolutely still, listening, but all you can hear is the rain hitting the window.

You turn to face him. There are raindrops on his yellow jacket. You pull the jacket to one side and rest your head on his chest. After a few moments you realise you can hear a noise like the windscreen wipers and you wonder if it's a kind of hypnagogic auditory hallucination or if it's the pulse in your temple.

You wake up in the original position you had occupied on the shared bed, facing away from him. A thin grey light from the window reveals large brown flowers on the wallpaper. You turn over and look at him. His face looks the same, smooth, unlined, eyes open. On his chest a line of stitching provides a point of detail on the otherwise featureless dark fabric that covers his frame and padding. Remembering the last thing that happened before you fell asleep, you press your ear to his chest. It's faint, but still there, but again, it could be the blood in your own head. Or it could be auto-suggestion.

You go into the bathroom and run the shower. When you come out, I'm sitting up on the edge of the bed staring at the floor.

"Shall we go?"

You drive along the coast towards Zeebrugge.

"What did you buy from the DIY store?"

My voice is flat, affectless.

"I think you know."

We take a ferry to England and are then faced with a long drive to London. By the time we reach the M25, it's late. In Upper Holloway you park Hilde's car outside the kids' school. It's a very short walk to your house. I follow you up the path. The house is in darkness. The kids' rooms are empty, their cupboards and drawers bare. You offer me your bedroom and say you're going to sleep in your son's room.

In the morning, you look in on me, your face blank, and you say goodbye before going downstairs. I hear the chink of a glass as a drink is poured, then another, and finally the sound of the front door. I get up and watch from the window as you cross the street. You open the boot of the car and look inside. The plastic bag from the DIY store is still sitting there. You close the boot, then open the driver's door and get in.

I feel a tiny stabbing pain on the left side of my chest as I think about what might be in that bag and what it could be used for.

It's not long before the street becomes busy with parents dropping off their kids, some on foot, others by car. I watch you watching the street and the school gate. A large black car stops in the middle of the road and two children get out. A boy and a girl. The black car moves off and you get out of Hilde's car and call them. They stop and look at each other, then run towards you and I see you holding them close to you. A short conversation takes place and you open the rear door of the car and they look at each other again before getting in. You start the engine and pull out of the parking space. As you move off down the street I have a last glimpse of the children sitting in the back seat, their heads nodding with the movement of the car. When you reach the end of the street, you turn left.

How far will you go before you stop and open the boot? The outskirts of London? Somewhere more remote?

It's usually somewhere remote.

Dead End

A ragged scream tears through the leaden heat. He sees a fountain of blood erupt from a body torn in half. Hears—or imagines he hears—the nauseating grind of a siren. Flash of a dentist's overhead light. Muscles tensed to snapping point. Then the eyes, in close-up. James Garner's from *Grand Prix*, but they could be anybody's. They could be his.

He half-opens one eye. From under the brim of his straw hat, he watches a brown lizard with an orange stripe. It moves across the pebbly path like an illuminated message on a dot-matrix information board.

Arms and legs tingling in the direct sunlight, he hears footsteps on the pebbles, sees the lizard dart into the grass.

"Hello, my love," Isabel says as she bends down to deposit her book and towel on the sun lounger next to his.

He pushes the brim of the hat up a little. She leans over him, sarong falling open against her thigh. He watches his hand rise, his finger touching the exposed flesh. The weight of her breasts pulls against the elastic material of her tankini top.

"Coming for a swim?" she says, taking half a step back as a bee lumbers between them.

"No," he says, watching the bee. "I'm not much of a swimmer."

"I love swimming." She backs away, unwinds the sarong.

He hears her enter the pool, one careful step at a time, then the sound of her pushing forward into the water, arms outstretched. The physical reaction he'd had to their momentary closeness begins to subside, and then returns as he pictures her body moving though the water.

He pokes at the brim of his hat so that he can watch the movement of the top of her back and pale shoulders as she swims. He can't make them out at this distance, but she has the faintest freckles on her shoulders and back. The first time he saw them, as he and Isabel undressed each other in her bedroom on a weekday afternoon, he had traced his finger over the random patterns.

They hadn't had long; he'd been expected home.

When she reaches the far end and turns around to come back, the kicking of her legs splashes pool water on to a bricked-up doorway in the nearest wall.

He looks at the doorway. At some stage in the past it had, presumably, led somewhere.

After a while, he realises the noises have stopped.

"It's thirsty work this, darling," he hears her say.

He smiles and gets up from the sun lounger. The garden of the house is criss-crossed by paths, some of which lead only to flower beds. He takes one that he knows leads to the house, passing between two beds of lilac festooned with butterflies and abuzz with bees. He walks under the archway and enters the *gîte*, which is attached to the side of the main house. He pours a glass of orange juice and returns the carton to the fridge, then looks at the glass he has poured and picks it up. Condensation forms on the outside of the glass as sweat runs down into the small of his back. He lifts the glass to his mouth.

The glass now half-empty, he places it back on the work surface and stares absently at the wall behind the wicker-work sofa in the lounge area of their studio room. There's a watercolour in a gilt frame above the right-hand end of the sofa and a curtain hanging from a rail covering the wall behind the left-hand end. He approaches the sofa and pulls the curtain to one side. Behind it is a glass-panelled door with another curtain on the other side—in the main house.

In his pocket his phone vibrates. He takes it out to find a text from his daughter.

Hi Dad. I swam 10 lengths ☺ xx

He smiles as his index finger picks out his reply.

Well done darling. More than I can manage! xx

He stares at the curtain behind the sofa again, his smile fading.

He returns to the garden with a fresh glass of orange juice to find Isabel floating on her back in the pool absolutely still.

"I don't know how you do that," he says, appraising the outline of her body in the water.

"It's easy."

"I couldn't do it."

"Anyone can do it."

"Not me," he says. "Not without moving my arms and legs."

She keeps her legs together and her arms outstretched and lies perfectly still.

He smiles at her as sweat runs from his hairline.

He kneels down, placing the glass of orange juice by the edge of the pool. Isabel turns on to her front and kicks out behind. She approaches the side, her fingers alighting on the tiled rim. He covers her hand with his and she smiles up at him. He looks down at her breasts, wondering if his sunglasses will conceal his wandering eyes, but knowing they won't. He feels a tightening in his shorts.

"I want you," he says.

Her lips part. She grabs his wrist and is about to try to pull him into the water.

"My phone," he says, resisting.

There's a hoarse scream or a cry from somewhere beyond the confines of the garden. It sounds like an animal in sudden, unbearable pain. It sounds like the same scream that he has heard before.

"What *is* that?" he asks.

"A donkey?" she suggests. "Every time I hear it, I think it's being sawn in half."

"I know how it feels," he says.

Her face hardens; she looks down, her grip on his wrist abruptly relaxing. Then she lets go and drops beneath the surface. She twists around under water and when she kicks to propel herself away from the side of the pool, she gives him a good soaking.

He takes his phone from the pocket of his shorts and places it on the nearest sun lounger, then removes his sunglasses and puts them down next to the phone. He checks her position and dives in.

With his eyes closed he reaches for her as he moves under water. She twists away, trying to free herself from his grasp, but he holds on. They surface and he rubs his eyes.

"I'm sorry," he says, gasping for breath. "I'm sorry. Really. It was a silly thing to say and it's not even true."

She struggles a bit more, but he senses the fight has gone out of her.

"I'm sorry," he says again, and he moves her hair out of her face as they tread water. He draws his legs up and encircles her waist, tightening his grip, but she tips forward, taking them both under water. His protest emerges in a stream of bubbles.

Isabel is lying on her back on a sun lounger. He is standing a few feet away, wondering if it's forgivable to have sex in a swimming pool. The sun has already dried the remaining droplets of water from her legs, and now the dark patches on her tankini—which she has put back on, since they don't know when the owners might reappear—shrink even as he watches. She is breathing regularly and he thinks she might be asleep.

He passes under the archway to the front of the property. Their hire car stands on the gravel drive. To the left, the single-track lane leads back to the road, the only route to Villefranche de Rouergue. To the right, the lane peters out into a cinder track, which runs into a high hedge. He remembers when they came out for a walk the night before, hearing the creatures in the fields and hedgerows. The churring and chirruping of birds, he had said; the chiming of cicadas, Isabel had thought. He wonders who was right.

He looks down the lane, which Isabel had described as a cul-de-sac. He had pointed out that the phrase, although French, was not used by the French. So the phrase itself was a linguistic cul-de-sac, *n'est-ce pas?*

"Not so much cul-de-sac as *mise-en-abîme*, in that case," he remembers her saying.

He stares into the distance, the skin under his right eye twitching.

In his pocket, his phone vibrates for an incoming text message.

They are in Villefranche, walking through streets of grey stone.

"We could be in Yorkshire," he says, taking her hand and enjoying the warm, damp hollow of her palm.

"Except for the sub-tropical conditions," she says.

"And the French graffiti," he adds, pausing by a stencil of a skull signed, apparently, "TOMBO". "And the brasseries and patisseries, and the smell of Gauloises et cetera."

By mutual consent they turn down an alley that looks as if it will offer another way out. It doesn't. They stand and face one another at the end of the alley, each taking the other's hand, and kiss.

Eventually the medieval town surrenders its main square and they wander around the market. He stays by her side, either holding her hand or touching the back of it. Sometimes their legs come into contact and he presses against her hips, whispering into her ear. She smiles and makes faint noises of pleasure and encouragement.

She stops at a stall selling a variety of dry sausages.

"What's '*myrte*'?" he asks, pointing to one labelled "*avec myrte*".

"Myrtle, I expect. Sounds delicious."

"I know what '*cochon*' is," he says, looking at another label. "What about '*âne*'?"

"Donkey," she says, catching his eye, before they both turn to look at the looped sausage, a deep reddish brown colour speckled with chalky white mould.

"That explains a lot," he says.

They stop in a café for a glass of wine, then walk back slowly to where they had left the car, parked in a line of vehicles overlooking the railway station. There is a languid quality to Isabel's movements that he finds exquisitely erotic and as he lowers himself into the driver's seat he finds that he is aroused. She fans herself as he starts the engine and he buzzes down her window as well as his own.

The houses lining the road soon fall away and he changes down to second as dictated by the gradient, the car traversing the contours, first one way then the other, to reach higher ground. As they turn left on to the narrow lane down to the hamlet he unclips his seat belt and allows it to loop back on to its spool. She looks at him and raises her eyebrow.

"Last time you waited until we were half way down the lane," she says.

"I'm relaxing," he says with a smile.

Together in the kitchen they prepare ingredients for dinner.

"Is the sun over the yard arm?" she asks.

"Pretty much."

He opens the fridge and takes out a bottle of wine and a beer. He pours a glass of wine and passes it to her.

"Cheers," they both say.

He pours his beer into a glass. He's always done this since reading in a magazine that being able to smell your beer as you drink it enhances your enjoyment.

He tops up Isabel's wine glass and takes the empty bottles outside and stands them with the others that have accumulated by the side of the *gîte*. At the end of the week, if not before, he will take them into Villefranche and recycle them. As he looks at the line of bottles standing to attention he suddenly has a very clear memory of his son asking him why, when he had swept up a broken wine glass at home, he had dumped the broken glass in the regular bin rather than the recycling bin for glass, metal and plastic. He had told his son that he believed broken glass couldn't go in the recycling, but had to go in the general waste, and his son had asked about bottles breaking when being dropped in the recycling bin. Was that a problem, he had asked? Did those broken bottles then have to be fished out of the recycling? He hadn't answered, he now realises. Something else had happened, some distraction had intervened, and they had all moved on and the question had remained unanswered, and he now realises that it's not that the wine glass is broken that's important, but that it's a different kind of glass, and he feels an urgent need to tell his son, to explain, so that when his son eventually finds out one day, perhaps from someone else, the truth about glass, he won't think back and remember how his father misled him. Lied to him, really. He wants to text him now, his son, text him and tell him about the different types of glass, but it further occurs to him that he doesn't really know enough about it. He doesn't know why the fact that it's a different kind of glass is so important. Surely glass is glass. Surely it all gets melted down and remade, doesn't it? What does it matter if some of it is thin and clear while some of it is green or brown and quite a bit thicker? Although not that much thicker—it depends on the type of glass.

He becomes aware of Isabel standing in the doorway of the *gîte* with an anxious expression on her face.

"Darling, what's wrong?" she says, approaching him now, arms outstretched. "Why are you crying?" She wipes his tears away. "Darling, darling," she murmurs as she holds him.

In the morning they need bread.

"I'll go. You stay in bed," he says.

"No, I want to come with you."

He tries to persuade her to stay, but she refuses.

It's warm but hazy. The haze will have burnt off by the time they get back from Villefranche with the bread.

They park in the same spot overlooking the railway station. Isabel is wearing a white short-sleeved top that gapes at the front when she leans forward. That she appears innocent of intent and oblivious to any effect only makes the effect all the more powerful.

"This is our space," she says.

"I don't like to drive any further in," he says. "Feels like there's no way out. That one-way system."

When they return to the car carrying a baguette and a bag containing two *pains aux raisins*, he fastens his seatbelt but then unclips it almost as soon as they start climbing the hill out of town. Isabel looks at him with that same raised eyebrow.

"Feeling even more relaxed?" she says.

He just smiles.

When they get back, they are standing on the gravel drive when a familiar scream rips open the now vivid blue stillness of the morning.

He turns and looks at her and pulls a sad face, then looks away at the line of empty bottles standing against the wall of the *gîte*. A bee investigates the neck of one bottle after another, then seems to have a better idea and veers off towards the garden.

He walks around to stand behind her and threads his arms through hers, around her waist, then allows his hands to settle on her wide hips. She leans her head back against his shoulder.

"I think I need a lie down," he says, taking her hand.

He's undressed her before they reach the bed. He kneels down and kisses the gentle swell of her tummy, tasting salt, chlorine, sun cream. He runs his hand down over her leg, almost but not quite making contact. She makes a low sound that tells him she likes what he's doing. He stands up and steps out of his shorts, feeling the weight of his phone in the pocket as he throws them the short distance to the armchair. She lies down on the bed and he goes to lie down next to her and he asks himself if he will be able to lose himself in the moment, or the next series of moments, or if he will be visited by thoughts of his children, if he'll be interrupted by the buzz of his phone's text alert, if he'll be assailed by worries about the hopelessness of the situation in which they find themselves, if he'll be distracted by images, which he realises just at that moment have begun to crowd in on him in the last few days, of dead ends. But, in spite of these thoughts and worries and images, he finds he can actually lose himself in the moment, because, from the first moment he touched her, from the first moment they kissed, he has known there is something unprecedented and different and unique about that touch and that kiss. What he feels for her is overpowering and he senses it's the same for her and she has told him it's the same for her and together they seem to have found something that means something profound to each of them, to both of them, and this meaning appears to be communicable by touch. They want each other, they desire each other, and when he is making love to her—which he is doing right now, right this very moment, and even his being aware of it is not enough to break the spell—it feels, it really feels as if he is doing something, going somewhere, feeling something he has never done before or been before or felt before. He knows it's the oldest feeling in the world, or one of them certainly, but to him, and to her, he thinks, it feels brand new, it feels like nothing they've ever felt before, like something they've never done before, it feels like somewhere neither of them has ever been before. Above all it feels like they are going to this place, performing this act and experiencing this feeling together and at the same time and even as he experiences it he thinks it feels like an out-of-body experience despite the fact it's all about his body and her body and their two bodies coming together and even this awareness does not impinge on the sensation or adulterate his happiness and even that word somehow does not have the undesired effect he so feared, when really you would expect it might, and he thinks to himself that it's a little bit like climbing a mountain, as you keep climbing and you see the summit disappearing ahead of you, a series of false summits, and then you see the real summit just a short way ahead and you know there's no way you're not going to make it and you do make it and you stop and look beyond and the view is the most amazing view you have ever seen and it's the first time you have seen it, this particular view, and it is in no way disappointing or predictable, but is breathtakingly beautiful and bathed in some impossible golden light and even as you think this, even as you think it's the most banal cliché ever to have entered your head, even as you think this, the vision doesn't darken or start to break up or become unstable, but persists, and a new feeling comes over him, one of great calmness, a feeling he can't remember experiencing for a long time, a calmness that fills him like the tide fills an estuary. And while they lie together on the bed and the sweat dries on their skin, he doesn't worry about his children or even about his wife, he doesn't worry that he and Isabel might be heading down a dead end, he doesn't worry about the screams of the donkey or the premonitory dream of the siren or the close-up of the terrified driver's eyes in the film he would for some reason always be reminded of when he went to the dentist as a child, he doesn't worry about the bee that will return to the empty bottles lined up outside the *gîte* and, attracted by the sticky residue inside one of them, probably one of his empty beer bottles, stumble inside and perhaps become stuck in that residue, and he doesn't worry that later when he loads up the car with the recycling he will fail to notice the bee inside the bottle and he doesn't think for a moment that when he releases his seat belt only a short way into the journey into town and Isabel raises her eyebrow at him that he might be about to need his seatbelt when the bee becomes unstuck at the bottom of the bottle and bumbles out of the bottle into the car and barges about, a bee in a car seeming so much bigger than normal, the size of a bat or a bird, and the interior of the car seeming so much smaller than normal, like the interior of a car *after* a horrific accident rather than before.

Maths Tower

The Maths Tower was built in 1969. Two hundred and forty-six feet high. Seventy-five metres. Thirty-six years later, a girl called Nina is sitting in Manchester Museum, across the road from the Maths Tower, watching at the window. Nina's parents enrolled as students in 1984. They met in the Maths Tower. One plus one equals two. Eight months later, in 1985, they scored over ninety per cent in their first-year exams and celebrated in a quiet corner on the fifth floor. Nine months on, four days early, Nina was born. She hadn't been planned and the strain broke them apart. Nina's father simply deducted himself from the equation and Nina's mother found it hard to cope. The sums didn't add up. Eighty pounds for a gram. Ten quid for twenty minutes. Two months in Styal prison. Nina went through eight foster homes in half as many years. When she started school she could barely count to three.

Fifteen years later, aged nineteen, she's a daily visitor to the museum, parting the curtains in the Ancient Egyptian room. She spends twice as long with these mummies as she did with her own. But her attention is fixed on the activity across the street. The scaffolding went up in the spring and plastic sheeting followed it, stretched like skin around the outside of the steel poles. Two hundred and six bones make up the human skeleton. If you jumped from the top of the Maths Tower you'd break at least half of them. When the tower is completely sheathed, the magic trick is ready. Slowly the covering is peeled back, from the top down, day by day, to reveal that the tower within has vanished. The trick takes a couple of weeks. Nina watches every day as a fine haze envelops the sheathed structure. Then the remaining plastic is removed in one go and the scaffold seems to tighten its joints and dig into the stump of the tower, an exoskeleton turning on its freight. The hard hats swarm, the orange vehicles growl and churn through the mud. The ever-shortening tower mutates. A caricature of a Balkan house, upper storeys overhanging. An air traffic controllers' observation deck. An East Berlin watchtower. When a yellow articulated arm reaches up dinosaur-like to close pincer jaws on concrete, a redundant tuft of steel cable springs forth like a sheared fan of muscle fibres—and with it billows a small cloud of tiny numbers.

Each new bite the mechanical jaws take out of the building releases another puff of digits, floating like seeds on the wind. It seems they are what held the tower together and now they are out in the world. A "2" lands on the front of a passing bus, which slows down and takes the next turning, following a new route. The wind blows a "4" on to the blue shirt of a football fan walking by, changing the identity of his favourite player. A geography student gives her mobile number to a boy she met the night before, but when he texts her later the message will be received by a female paramedic attending an emergency call.

Nina studies the ground at the foot of the tower. Each workman's boot that strikes the earth detonates a tiny explosion of numbers. Long strings of figures smoke out of the mountains of rubble and twist into the air where they cross the sky like banners pulled by invisible planes. Misconnections abound across the city as phone numbers on adverts and signs are replaced by those for petrochemical companies in Abu Dhabi and exclusive escort agencies operating Cheshire-wide out of Prestbury.

Numerical chaos reigns throughout the autumn. The remains of the tower are gradually razed and by December the diggers are crisscrossing level ground, over and over, round and round, trampling the remaining digits into the dirt. Nina lifts her eyes and stares through the faint haze where the tower once stood, until it finally dissipates in the cold, bright sunshine and all she can see are the snow-capped hills of the Peaks in the distance.

The Cellar

We know this much. We know that Stephen returns to the flat with his bike. It's not the first time he's brought the bike to the flat. But it's the first time he's stood outside, hesitating, not quite sure what to do. The time before, he chained it up outside, but it's raining tonight, a fine drizzle that will soak into his bicycle seat and take days to dry out. We assume he's wondering about taking the bike into the house and leaving it in the communal hallway, but he's met the guy who lives in the downstairs flat. He met him the first time he came to the flat on his own and the guy was standing in the doorway and Stephen had to ask him to let him by. *I live here*, Stephen had offered by way of explanation, *in Flat 5*, and it hadn't sounded convincing even to him. The guy from the downstairs flat had grudgingly stood to one side and made a point of telling Stephen about the bins. How if you put the wrong ones out on the wrong week, they wouldn't empty them. Stephen has noticed, since then, not that people have been putting the wrong bins out on the wrong week, but that someone has been putting the wrong things in the wrong bins. Yoghurt pots in the bin for plastic bottles, plastic bags in the bin for paper and cardboard. He wonders if the guy from the downstairs flat is one of those who puts the wrong things in the wrong bins.

Even we think the guy from the downstairs flat looks like the kind of person to complain about a bike left in the hallway, and Stephen's bike is too heavy to carry up to the top floor, where there is a convenient landing by the door to his flat. So, instead, he wheels it around the outside of the building to the back. Past a load of cigarette ends in a pile beneath the side window belonging to the downstairs flat. We feel certain that Stephen pictures the guy from the downstairs flat standing by his window smoking some relatively cheap brand and eventually dropping his filters outside on to the path, his girlfriend hovering somewhere in the flat behind him, sniffing the air pointedly.

At the back of the house is a series of poorly maintained steps leading down to the cellar. Can you see it? Can you picture it, we should say? Stephen leaves his bike at the top while he goes down. The steps are furred with moss and the floor, over which the cellar door scrapes, is gritty and uneven. He has been down here once before, but without his bike. He'll be remembering it, the complicated layout of the rooms, the requirement to duck his head, the fact a bare bulb is permanently left on. (You can see he doesn't like the cellar. Even before what's about to happen to him he doesn't like it. He seems vaguely suspicious of it, almost offended by it.) This time, the cellar is in darkness. We see him flick the switch by the door and nothing happens. We see him move into the first room and then veer to the left, ducking his head, half from memory, half because the grainy light admitted by the open door tells him he needs to. He moves through the second room and turns right through the open doorway into the third room, where he remembers, just in time, to duck again. Then, just beginning to straighten up, he hears a loud thud and a tearing sound and he bends his knees and holds his head. He holds his head and keeps very still. He is waiting for the numbness to pass and the pain to kick in. He presses his hand hard against the wound, afraid to remove his woollen beanie. At least the hat is dark and any blood won't show. Any blood? Oh there will be blood. The wound throbs. We imagine he feels anger that this obstacle, which he has not yet seen, was not here on his first visit to the cellar. Someone has moved something or some building work has been done, but no one has bothered to make it safe or replace the bulb. He gets out his phone, while remaining crouched down, and shines a light at the ceiling. There's a long, narrow section hanging down lower, roughly plastered, presumably a consequence of the property's conversion into flats. Maybe it conceals pipes or something like that. But it wasn't there the last time he was down in the cellar, he's certain of that. Can we say he's certain of that? Let's assume we can. Let's give ourselves permission to make certain assumptions. He's certain it wasn't there last time he was in the cellar. How stupid someone must have been to do this work and not make sure one of the tenants would not walk into it. His head is throbbing more and more now. He'll be remembering the thud, the tearing sound. Go on: he *is* remembering the thud, the tearing sound. He's thinking to himself how when you hit something hard without meaning to—your head, for instance—it really does make a sickening sound. He feels sick now as he remembers the thud and the sound of skin tearing. He doesn't want to remove his hat. He'll be thinking he deserves this. Is that too much of a leap? We don't think so. He deserves it. *We're* not saying that. We're only saying that's what he'll be thinking. That he deserves it. For what he's done. He deserves this and a lot more.

There's a noise now, a rushing noise like a high wind between buildings, but deeper, more mechanical. He won't know what it is, but he doesn't like it. He shines the light of his phone again. There's not much to see. Electricity meters. Gas meters. One for each flat. Pipes, pillars and plaster. Cobwebs. Great black swags of cobwebs hanging from the walls and ceiling—the extremely low ceiling. Exposed brickwork. An old boiler.

He'll be wondering if the rushing noise is in his head, if he's done some permanent damage to his hearing or his brain.

He retreats at a crouch. He doesn't want to bang his head again. He finds his way back to the steps and climbs up out of the cellar. He's not taking his bike down there. There are some railings at the back of the house. He could chain it to them. So what if the seat gets wet? He doesn't care about that right now. But he knows he'd care about it if it happened.

So he walks his bike round to the front of the building, heaves it up the steps and lets himself in. He leans his bike against the hall wall, then goes back to shut the door and presses the timer for the light. There's some post for him, a bill, on the hall table. He grabs it and heads for the stairs. The light goes out before he reaches the top of the building, like it always does.

Once inside his flat he stands in front of the mirror and starts to remove his hat. He takes it very slowly. He can feel resistance where flesh and wool have become enmeshed. Gingerly he teases them apart and removes the hat. There is a gash on top of his shaved head, about three inches long. It extends down over his forehead. He leans close to the mirror and pulls the sides of the wound apart to see how deep it is, if it needs stitches. He decides not. But it hurts.

He washes it, takes paracetamol and ibuprofen and goes to bed.

In the middle of the night he is woken by a noise, a sort of rushing noise. His head is throbbing. He doesn't know why. He's forgotten. He manages to get back to sleep.

We don't know what he dreams about, but we're willing to bet he dreams about us. We're willing to bet he dreams about the cellar.

When he wakes up, it's light and there's blood on his pillow and for a moment he doesn't know why, and then he remembers. He gets up and runs a bath, makes a cup of tea. He looks at his head in the mirror, but realises that looking at it makes it hurt more, or makes him more anxious about it, or just reminds him of the moment it happened. The thud, the tearing sound, the rushing noise.

He sees his beanie on the sofa and reaches for it. He peers inside and picks little bits of skin out of it.

He lies in the bath. Because there is no window in the bathroom there is an extractor fan that comes on if he tugs the light cord. He doesn't like the insistent noise it makes, which seems out of proportion to the job it's required to do, so he tends to bathe with the light off and the door ajar. Sometimes he lights little candles, but not this morning. He reclines, allows the back and top of his head to go under the water. He lies like that for a while, staring up at the grubby artexed ceiling, thinking of the bathroom back at the house, its skylight and white enamel bath, contrasting with this cream plastic tub. He's done the right thing. He knows he has. This transitional period, this interim phase, was always going to be difficult. And less so for him than for others.

He slides down in the bath, submerging himself, pushing air down through his nostrils. He holds his position, feeling momentarily safe. He can hear his heartbeat under water—and something else. Some other noise growing in volume. A kind of rushing noise.

He resurfaces and wipes his eyes before opening them and sees immediately that the bathroom is darker. He looks at the door, which is still ajar but is not admitting the light it was admitting before. The wall to the right of the door, which would normally reflect a little of the light from the main room, is dark. The rushing noise is loud in his head. He reaches out from the bath and catches the edge of the door with his fingers. He pulls it all the way open and doesn't understand what he sees. The main room is dark when it should be light. It's so dark he can't make anything out. He thinks that maybe somebody has erected scaffolding outside the window and shrouded it in opaque plastic—that's the kind of thing he thinks, probably, in less than a second—but he can't even see the window. Although the bath is warm, he suddenly feels quite cold. He pulls the towel off the radiator and steps out of the bath, wrapping the towel around him and standing in the doorway. As he stares into the main room, his eyes slowly become accustomed to the darkness and he realises there is a little light coming from the kitchen, off to the left, which allows him to make out various details in the gloom of the strangely altered main room of his studio flat. He sees a bank of electricity meters, some gas meters, what looks like an old boiler. There's a bare-brick pillar in the middle of the room. Over to the right-hand side, there's an obstruction hanging down from the ceiling.

He hears the rushing noise.

He reaches his hand into the room, feeling for the light switch, but the wall on the left where it should be is damp and crumbly to the touch. There is no light switch. Only cobwebs and decaying plaster.

He backtracks into the bathroom and sits on the floor, resting against the side of the bath and pulling his knees up to his chin, staring out into the darkness. After a moment, the rushing noise gets louder and louder in his ears, like a river in full spate, and he pushes the door to. Then he closes the door and locks it and when he opens it again some time later—ten minutes, half an hour, maybe longer?—the flat has returned to normal.

He cycles back to the house in the middle of the next day. There is no car in the drive. He uses his key to unlock the door. He leaves his bike in the hall. There are no downstairs neighbours here. The house is quiet. It's a work day, a school day.

We see him sit on the bottom step and remove his shoes before walking upstairs. On the landing he lifts the lid of the laundry basket and takes out the dirty things, making three piles on the carpet—blacks, coloureds, whites. He enters one of the two bedrooms either side of the bathroom. He picks up the T-shirts and the socks and the football top and drops them on their respective piles on the landing. He makes the bed, piles the exercise books neatly on the desk. We suppose he does this to make himself feel better. But why does anybody do anything? As he leaves the bedroom, it goes dark, as if he's switched the light off, but it's the middle of the day and he didn't touch the light switch. The rushing sound is back. Standing on the landing, he turns and looks into the room he's just left. The gas and electricity meters, the exposed brick, the great hanging drapes of sooty cobwebs.

He stumbles into the bathroom. He rests the weight of his upper body on the sink and looks into the hollow eyes of the face in the mirror. What will he be thinking? That his eyes look haunted, even hunted? In his head is the rushing noise—like a tidal race, a swarm of bees, a needlessly revved engine, a leaf-blower, an extractor fan.

He goes back to the landing and ventures into the bedroom on the other side of the bathroom, where he scoops up knickers, a school blouse, inside-out tights. Back on the landing, he gathers the piles of dirty clothes. He glances in the first bedroom as he makes for the top of the stairs. He sees what he ought to see—a made bed, floor empty of discarded clothes, table covered with piles of school books.

He loads the machine in the cellar and sets it going. We look at this cellar with its intact plaster and its functioning boiler, its white goods and neatly stacked cardboard boxes. He switches the light off and leaves the room. We hear his footsteps on the stairs going back up to the ground floor.

He cycles back to the flat. The wind rushes past his ears. A familiar sound. He glances behind him, but the road is empty.

He leaves the bike in the hall. The guy from the downstairs flat has not complained yet. He presses the timer switch and gets most of the way up to his flat before the light goes off. He lets himself in and locks the door behind him. He gets some lunch, does a little work, moving from the kitchen to the main room, to the bathroom when necessary. Maybe the cupboard in the hall, where he hangs his clothes on hangers left by the previous tenant, her size fluctuating between fourteen and sixteen. His copy of Roland Topor's novel *The Tenant* is among the books he has brought over from the house. It's years since he read it and he's not in a hurry to read it again.

He goes back to the house to hang the washing out and then returns to the flat. As he climbs the stairs, he appears to be listening out for something, but his expression of silent concentration doesn't change. He unlocks the door to his flat and everything inside looks normal. He makes a cup of tea and sits on the sofa to drink it. The sofa, like everything else, is a perfect fit for the space where he has put it. The futon. The desk. The coffee table and sofa. Perfect. Everything just right. It doesn't matter about people putting the wrong things in the wrong bins and the guy from the downstairs flat dropping his cigarette ends out of the window. The flat feels good; his stuff fits.

When he tilts his head back to drink, his head hurts. He puts his hand up to the wound, which has started to scab over.

He puts the mug in the kitchen and packs an overnight bag. At the door he stands and looks back at the flat before leaving. Everything looks normal. There's no rushing sound. His head itches.

He cycles to the station, locks his bike up and waits on the platform. The train trundles out of the city and races through the countryside. Where are we while all this is going on? Don't worry, we're not far away. He looks out of the window, thinking about where he is going, no doubt, who he is going to see. There is a constant rushing sound, but that will be the train, he thinks. He looks in the windows at the backs of houses next to the line. We could be behind any of them.

He gets off the train and takes the underground. He stands by the open window between the carriages. There is a loud rushing noise. We could be in the next carriage, but he doesn't look round. He gets off the tube and walks the rest of the way. He lets himself in; they've swopped keys to their respective flats. Her flat is empty. There is no noise, just the sounds of the street. He makes a drink, does some work, sits and waits. He looks up at every sound. He gets to his feet and checks the bedroom, the kitchen, the bathroom, even the back stairs. Nothing. He stops and looks at the framed Magritte print on the landing. A man listens to a gramophone while a woman's body lies on the couch behind him. Three identical men watch from the balcony or from beyond the balcony, and another two lie in wait in the foreground. *L'assassin menacé.*

He stands in a central spot on the landing from where he can keep an eye on all rooms of the flat at the same time. His head hurts.

Later she comes home and holds him and says she loves him and he tells her he loves her and he starts to relax, but his head still hurts.

In the morning he leaves. He gets the underground and then the train. He picks up his bike and returns to the house, where he does some jobs that need doing, then gets back on his bike and cycles to the flat, the wind rushing in his ears. He thinks about the Magritte print. The three men at the window. The two men in the foreground waiting with a cudgel and a net. The murderer is ready to go, his hat and coat on a chair, his bag packed, but still he takes the time to listen to the gramophone. When he does go, you suspect, he will not get far. He will not escape justice; he will be judged. For the time being, though, he is taking pleasure in listening to music.

He reaches the flat and hesitates, as if thinking about coming round to the back of the building, perhaps to confront his fear of the cellar. But instead he unlocks the door, wheels his bike in and leans it against the wall. There is a letter on the hall table for Simone Choule, Flat 5. Presumably the former tenant. He picks it up and starts climbing the stairs, thinking about that name, Simone Choule. Where has he heard it before?

The light goes out before it would normally do so. Perhaps because he took a moment to pick up Simone Choule's letter? He is suddenly deafened by a loud noise, as if one of the tenants is playing industrial music and has opened his front door. But he can't see any spill of light from an open door. He can't see any of the doors. In fact he can't see anything at all. It does get very dark in the stairwell when the lights go off, the skylight being small and grimy. But we don't imagine he's kidding himself. He knows what's going on. He reaches out for the wall, but it's crumbly damp plaster he feels, not woodchip wallpaper. He sways, unsure if the stairs are still stairs or a concrete floor. Perhaps he thinks if he tries to climb the stairs, if he believes they're still there and he can climb them, he'll reach the door to his flat. He gets out his phone and shines its dim light on a bank of electricity meters and a row of gas meters. Beyond them an old boiler. The rushing noise is getting louder and his head is throbbing. He tries to move forwards, as if drawn by something, though he doesn't know what. Maybe just the desire to reach the security of his flat. But it's like he can hear something. As if he can hear something over the roaring din. Something like a voice, calling his name perhaps, a woman's voice. Maybe the rushing abates a fraction and he can hear the voice through the gap, like suddenly hearing a human voice through a wall of radio static. And the voice is calling his name. *Stephen*, the voice is saying, *Stephen*. He falls to his hands and knees and crawls, ignoring the noise and the pain and concentrating only on the voice calling his name. He doesn't know if he's crawling uphill or down. He's just trying to get to the source of the voice. It feels to him—we imagine it feels to him—like the time he climbed a mountain and the wind was so strong and the gradient so steep and the ground so unsafe he was unable to remain upright and he had to crawl the last hundred yards with freezing fingers to reach the summit and the shelter of the cairn. He crawls until there's nowhere else to go and he feels something solid and heavy in the way. He feels upwards and there's the lock of his door beneath his fingertips. He takes out his keys and unlocks the door, climbing to his feet.

The door swings open and the noise behind him fades a little and he can hear a voice from inside.

Stephen?

It's her, he thinks, and he steps inside and closes the door.

Stephen?

It's dark in the flat although it's daytime. He suddenly feels cold. But then he realises the curtains have been drawn.

He thinks it's her, and it could be. But it could equally be us. It might even cross his mind to think of the men on

Magritte's balcony. They could be standing in a neat little row just behind the curtain.

Or maybe it is her. Maybe she thought she'd surprise him. Maybe she's the one who drew the curtains and is now lying waiting in bed. Maybe he's right about that and maybe he's done the right thing. Sooner or later, he'll find out.

The Reunion

On arrival, we'd had to wait behind a man in jumbo cords and a pastel polo shirt who was giving the receptionist a hard time about some problem in his room, a missing towel or a faulty light, and we formed an immediate impression of him that was somewhat negative. It wasn't long, however, before we realised he had a point.

They didn't have any record of our booking, despite having sent us an email of confirmation, which happily Maggie had printed out and brought along. So we had to fill in a form, holding up those who had arrived after us, and finally the girl behind the desk gave us a key card and a map. Yes, a map. It was a big hotel. A huge hotel. One of those places you get apparently in the middle of nowhere but actually no more than twenty miles from one or other dreary Midlands town. A former RAF training camp or stately home or converted mental asylum. This appeared to be all three, with not only west wings and east wings, but whole houses and vast halls tacked on to the main building. The room belatedly assigned to us was in one of the modern blocks. We walked along one edge of a grand, collonaded reception hall, past a tuxedoed piano player, through a little ante-room dominated by two stags' heads mounted on adjacent walls. We passed a bar with its shutter down, then turned right into a wide corridor.

The further we got from the main part of the hotel with its marble columns and wide, red-carpeted staircases, the shoddier and tattier everything became. There was an armchair in a corner that was missing a castor, a cabinet of drawers covered in scuff marks. I said to Maggie that it was like that scene in *Jacob's Ladder* where Tim Robbins is wheeled down into the bowels of a hospital that turns into a vision of hell with crazy people banging their heads against the wall and gobbets of bloody flesh lying around on the floor.

Maggie gave me her standard nod of impartial assent, the one kept for observations beyond her frame of reference. I realised, though, that if I was overly critical of the hotel, and therefore, by extension, of the evening itself, it could provoke a reaction. This was Maggie's evening—a medical school reunion—and the fact that I had readily agreed to come along meant that if at any point I regretted my decision, it would not be fair to allow it to show. As we trailed past a rather tired series of framed prints of the hotel in its heyday, I felt the raised glands in my neck. The prints on the wall were undated and there were no outward signs that would enable you to assign them to a particular period. They were like idealisations or artist's impressions. One hung askew and I wanted to straighten it, but I sensed Maggie's impatience to get to the room and so left it.

We pushed through a set of glass doors and found ourselves in a lobby area. There was a lift to our right, a corridor behind wood-panelled doors beyond that, and another corridor heading off from the far side of the lobby. An old-fashioned three-piece suite occupied the middle of the space. Facing the lift doors was a walnut table that had seen better days. On it was a folded copy of the *Independent*.

It appeared that we had to go up two floors; I'm not very good at waiting around for lifts. Or buses. Or anything that you suspect might never come.

"I'll take the stairs," I said, "and I'll still get there before you."

I took Maggie's bag in my spare hand and shouldered open the door to the stairs. I ran up one flight, barged through the equivalent door on the next floor and found myself in an identical lobby space. I pressed the call button and while wondering if the lift would ever arrive tried on a number of expressions. It was certainly taking its time, the lift. On a walnut table that was indistinguishable from the one on the floor below was another copy of the *Independent* folded in the same manner. I thought to myself it had been a waste of money my buying one that morning. When the lift arrived, the doors trundled open to reveal Maggie and a middle-aged couple, who looked as though they wanted to get out. She introduced them to me as Henrik and Caroline. I thought I could see a slightly guarded look in Henrik's eyes as we swopped places; Caroline looked as if, like Maggie, she just wanted to get to their room. Henrik had been a contemporary, Maggie told me as the lift doors closed behind me and I turned to press the button. He'd seemed a lot older than me, but then Maggie is four years my senior and some men age worse than others.

The interior of the lift was mirrored on three sides, which created a theoretically endless series of reflections in both side walls. I checked myself out. I wasn't ageing too badly. My problems were *inside* my head. I knew that. Maybe physiologically, certainly mentally.

"You look beautiful," Maggie said in a way that managed to be affectionate and mocking at the same time.

When we finally got to our room, the third on the left beyond the wood-panelled doors, and managed to get the key card to flash green rather than red on the fifth attempt, we found we had one small towel between the two of us, no complimentary toiletries, and the shower produced either a trickle of boiling water or an icy torrent. I thought about helping Maggie out of her travelling clothes and suggesting we test out the mattress, but I sensed she wanted to get back downstairs for pre-dinner drinks as soon as possible. So while Maggie plugged in her hair-straighteners I stood to one side of the hot trickle in the shower cubicle pressing at my neck and trying to work out if the gland was bigger or smaller than the day before. I had mentioned it to Maggie and she had dismissed it. Ideally, this would have sufficed. Whereas the average person might think they had a cold coming on and the raised gland was their body's natural way of fighting it, my thoughts turn to leukaemia, lymphoma, Hodgkin's disease.

I leaned over the washbasin and wiped a swathe of condensation from the mirror so that I could see my reflection. I fancied that it was studying me rather than I it. If so, perhaps it felt sorry for me with my imaginary ailments and constant nagging anxiety. Or perhaps it just thought I was ridiculous. It wasn't bothered by anything like that. It was free.

Towelling myself dry, I returned to the bedroom, where Maggie was just stepping into her specially bought ball gown with its flatteringly high waist and gratifyingly plunging neckline. I slipped into my oversize dead man's DJ and a pair of highly polished shoes that were coming away from their soles. We left the room and headed back to the lifts. I suggested we walk down and Maggie acquiesced. She looked good in the ballgown and I thought she would prefer to watch the movement of the dress over her long legs than stand around waiting for the lift that might never arrive. I knew that was my preference. I pushed open the door to the stairwell and ushered Maggie through. As we walked down, a small party in tuxedos and ball gowns was coming up. They passed us and turned left. They were going in the right direction, but they were on the wrong level.

"They're going the wrong way," I whispered to Maggie.

But as I made the remark, I lost confidence in its content.

"Are you going to the reunion?" I asked the disappearing party while they were still within earshot.

"Yes," they said.

"It's this way," I said. "Down two flights. Unless you can get down at the other end?"

"No, this is the way," said a tall man with thinning hair and a perfectly fitting suit.

"How *can* it be?" I said to Maggie.

I pictured the two identical lobbies with their walnut tables and copies of the *Independent*. How had we gone wrong?

Maggie had stopped. We exchanged puzzled looks. The people who knew where they were going headed off while we dithered on the stairs. Eventually, I thought we might as well follow them. When we got as far as we could go and hadn't reached the main part of the hotel, and couldn't find another stairwell, *then* we could come back. So Maggie and I walked down the corridor, which was as similar to the one down which we had walked to get to our room as it was possible to be without actually being the same corridor. There would be no way out at the far end, and even if there was it would only be a stairway and we'd have to descend two flights to get to where we wanted to be.

Even the series of prints on the wall looked the same, one hanging askew. We passed a facsimile of the scuffed cabinet. I looked at the armchair in the corner. It sat unevenly due to a missing castor.

We entered a wide corridor and turned left at the end of it, past a bar that still had its shutters down. Then there was the room with the stags' heads, the piano player on the edge of the main reception hall (which was now heaving with well-dressed bodies) and we were back where we'd started, without having had to go down two floors. Maggie and I looked at each other in puzzlement and I just had time to start asking "What the fuck—" when a tall woman in a taffeta ball gown swept past and dragged Maggie off to meet someone else she hadn't seen for twenty years.

They were giving out drinks. The choice was champagne or orange juice. I wandered off to a bar in an adjoining room where I waited behind a fat man who was ordering two turkey sandwiches. Back on the fringes of the main room where the welcome drinks were still being served, I stood with a pint of Guinness—the nearest I could get to something drinkable—and looked on. At the far side of the room I could see Maggie laughing generously at somebody's joke, her head dropping forward so that her straightened hair fell in front of her face. I became aware of a tall, slim man with silver hair standing near to me. A picture of understated elegance, in his own tailored suit and carefully polished shoes, he sipped at a glass of champagne.

"It's strange being an outsider at one of these events," he said with an almost imperceptible turn of the head.

"Very strange," I agreed. "Will," I added, offering him my hand.

"Gordon," he said with a warm smile.

We raised our glasses to our lips and watched the increasingly animated crowd in the centre of the room.

"Do you know," he began, "I was reading in the paper today—just now, upstairs, in fact—that during the Cold War the East Germans used to pay Bulgarian border guards for every East German they shot trying to cross the frontier into the West. It's almost unbelievable, isn't it?" He tipped the last of his champagne into his mouth and swallowed. "I don't know what made me think of that."

"Extraordinary," I agreed.

"I'm not sure I could kill anybody, even if ordered to do so."

"Not even for money?" I joked.

"Especially not for money," he said, turning to me. "Nice to meet you, Will. Excuse me."

As he walked away to look for his wife, I ticked myself off for my banal and unfunny joke.

I became aware of my fingers probing inside the collar of my dress shirt. I wondered if this latest fixation on head and neck cancers would end up with another referral to a specialist. I remembered with a jolt the not-so-smooth progress of the endoscope up my nose and down past my ear.

One of the organisers appeared up in the gallery with a photographer. Cupping her hands, the organiser announced a complicated sequence of group photographs. I took this as my cue to wander back to the bar and secure a second pint of Guinness. When I returned to the reception hall the photographer had finished. I looked for Maggie and saw her talking to a man with a paisley-patterned bowtie but when she lifted her head up to the light I saw it wasn't Maggie at all. The direct light revealed deeper lines, a less youthful skin texture. I felt a hand on my shoulder and turned around. *This* was Maggie, looking several years younger than the woman I'd thought was her. She introduced me to a well-meaning gastroenterologist from Peterborough and we had a conversation about five-a-side football. Despite both being regular players of the game, neither one of us was at all interested in what the other had to say.

Fortunately dinner was announced, so I was able to escape and find Maggie again and together we joined the throng heading towards the ballroom.

"I can't remember," I said to her, "is Jonathan coming to this?"

Maggie and Jonathan had met in their first year and started going out. They'd stayed together for a number of years, until a mutual acquaintance had lured Jonathan away from Maggie for a one-night stand that had turned into marriage, kids, the lot.

"No," Maggie answered, looking all around as she spoke, "this is not Jonathan's scene at all."

I wanted to say that it wasn't mine. It wasn't mine possibly even more than it wasn't Jonathan's. But I kept quiet. My hand crept up to my neck as we shuffled towards the seating plan resting on an easel by the entrance to the ballroom.

"No doubt we'll be on a table at the back," Maggie said, "with all the other people who booked at the last minute."

As we duly made our way towards the back of the ballroom, I had a look around. Two large video projection screens were each showing a series of stills, mugshots taken on enrolment. They were monochrome and the images had either become degraded or had been drenched with a sepia hue. There were probably two hundred, maybe three hundred people at the event; less than half of those would be partners, and possibly a not insignificant proportion of the partners would have been fellow students. I was trying to work out how long I might have to watch the parade of faces before Maggie's might appear. I had seen photographs of Maggie—and Jonathan—from back then. I was confident I'd recognise her. It's not as if the passage of twenty-five years actually makes you a different person. You just look a little older. Or a lot older.

I saw a picture of the organiser, the woman who had appeared on the balcony to orchestrate group photographs. She'd been slimmer, but you could already see the confidence in her eyes. For her it seemed a short step from enrolling to sending out invitations for a twenty-five-year reunion. She already knew she was going to do it. Maybe not explicitly, but she knew herself very well, she knew what she was capable of.

On the other screen I saw an early mugshot of the guy from the lift, Henrik, and he did indeed look a lot younger, but, again, the eyes were the same. That reticence, suspicion even.

I looked away from the mugshots in order to be introduced to the people at our table. Through a combination of first impressions, whispered intel from Maggie and the fruits of my own efforts at conversation, I gathered that they were a mixture of old friends of Maggie's and former fellow students: a likeable psychologist whose husband had left her for another man; a guy in his early fifties who had given up medicine for web design, but whose ideas seemed mired in the 1990s; a woman who had trained as a GP, before taking time out to have kids and finally going back to do a day a week; another part-time GP and editor of medical journals and his wife, a teacher who called herself a freelance journalist on the strength of writing a column for her husband's magazine about being married to a doctor.

When I next looked towards the front of the ballroom, there was Maggie's mugshot just fading from the screen on the left. I'd gathered now that the two screens were showing the same photographs, but out of sync. I saw the psychologist from our table. She was smiling at the camera, her eyes full of hope and expectation.

I turned back to the table, where three Polish waitresses in black and white costumes had converged. Drinks were being ordered, but the choice appeared to be limited to red or white, as far as I could tell from my attempts at dialogue with the three Poles, who, in terms of their mental and practical preparedness, were still on the plane from Warsaw.

"I'm going to the bar," I told Maggie.

I watched the faces fade in and fade out on the screens as I crossed the room. The last face I saw before the angle became too narrow to see anything at all made me come to an abrupt halt with a silly expression on my face.

Because it was mine.

I backtracked. The face that had looked a lot like mine twenty years earlier had gone and been replaced by that of

Gordon, the man I had met in the reception hall. I looked at the other screen, but it would be a while before the shot came around again and I'd be able to see it and realise that the guy who looked like me didn't look that much like me after all.

I stood waiting for the bartender to pour me a pint of Guinness. He tried to make conversation. He was Greek, very friendly, and he didn't have many customers, but I wasn't up for it. I felt strange, dissociated from my surroundings. I palpated my neck.

"Hello, Will," said a voice.

I turned around to see Henrik leaning on the bar. He asked the bartender for a Scotch. From the glassy look in his eyes I guessed he'd already had a couple.

"It's weird, isn't it?" he said.

"What?"

"This. This place. This whole evening. The mugshots. I didn't know they were going to do that. With that picture constantly flashing up on screen, it's like there's two of you. You now and you then. Do you know what I mean?"

"I saw yours," I said. "You've not changed a bit."

He gave a little laugh and knocked back his Scotch.

"I'm going to head back," I said.

"Cheers."

Seated at the table with the starters arriving, I waited for a gap in the conversation and turned to Maggie.

"What was going on with that whole lift thing?" I asked her.

"I can't explain it," she said, her eyes shining. "We went up but then didn't need to come down again. It's this place. The rules are different here."

I could tell Maggie was having a good time; she wouldn't normally come out with something like that. She's a very rational person. Either being a doctor made her like that or she became a doctor because that was the kind of person she was. Bit of both probably.

"Do you think it's possible," I said, "that we actually went down when we thought we were going up? After I got in?"

"But then we'd have just got back where we started and that wasn't the right floor. It's just—" She stopped and her eyes widened and she sang the theme tune to *The Twilight Zone*. I couldn't remember the last time she'd done that—perhaps ten years ago. I smiled and she leaned forward and I kissed her, then immediately she turned away and put her hand on the psychologist's arm to impart some fascinating piece of gossip she'd just remembered.

Thinking that it would be a while before the main course arrived, I got up from the table. On one of the big screens I recognised the sequence of mugshots that had preceded that of the guy who looked a bit like the younger me. When the face came up again, I studied it. Was he here, in the room? He would be four years older than me if he was Maggie's contemporary. Would he have aged better?

I thought of him as a version of me four years on, just as the second lobby I'd visited with the identical walnut table was a version of the one on the floor below. It was simply a floor higher. Separated in space rather than time.

I wondered if I should get another pint, but remembered I hadn't finished the last one.

On a table next to the easel just outside the ballroom was a laptop. It was playing a slideshow of the pictures taken in the hotel's reception hall. I picked out Maggie, smiling broadly and looking up at the camera just like everybody else. I saw the web designer and the boring gastroenterologist and even, standing on the edge of the group, Gordon, the man I had talked to briefly. I spotted Henrik and his wife, Caroline. There was the divorced psychologist, the tall man with the thinning hair who had known where he was going, there was the woman in taffeta and the man from the reception desk who had changed out of his jumbo cords and pastel polo shirt. And there, just to the left of centre, was I, my neck tendons straining with the effort of holding my head up to smile for the camera. Maybe I looked a little tired around the eyes, perhaps I appeared a tad heavier in the jowls, even slightly paunchier.

I turned around and headed back into the ballroom. I checked out the nearest tables, but there was no sign of anyone who looked a bit like me. I reached our table, but remained standing, scanning the room, running my eyes over every table in there. He wasn't to be seen. I sat down, thanked the waitress for my main course and smiled at Maggie, who still looked like she was having a good time.

"This is *so* weird," she said quietly but emphatically.

She didn't know how weird.

I pushed back my chair.

"Where are you going?" she asked.

"I won't be long."

"How's your neck?"

I looked at her.

"Are your glands still up?"

"I've just got to . . . "

My legs took me away from the table. I didn't like it when she didn't show concern, and I didn't like it when she did. She couldn't win, and neither could I. I prodded my neck as I crossed to the exit. I glanced at the group photo on the laptop, wondering, as I sometimes did, what was the point of a life like this, a life lived in constant fear of its ending. Wouldn't it just be easier to cut short the wait?

I fingered the keycard in my pocket with one hand and the raised gland in my neck with the other as I walked slowly and softly past the wonky chair and the scuffed cabinet. I stopped to straighten the print that was hanging askew.

The glass doors gave on to the lift lobby. The walnut table looked bare. Sitting on the shiny velveteen sofa reading the *Independent* was Gordon.

"Hello, Will," he said, turning the page.

I had no doubt that if I were to go up a floor, there he would be again sitting on the sofa reading the same newspaper. And whichever floor I was on, our room would be three doors down on the left beyond the wood-panelled doors.

I reached the door and slid the keycard into the slot. It flashed red. I tried again. Still red. I tried sliding it in very slowly and extracting it just as slowly. Still the red light flashed. I stood for a moment and listened to my breathing, which was fast and shallow. And then I heard a man's voice. It was very close. I looked behind me to see if someone had left their door open. They'd left the ballroom to make a phone call and decided to do it in the privacy of their room. But the doors on the other side of the corridor were all shut and the corridor was empty. Sometimes, when I play five-a-side football and we're warming up while waiting to begin, I count the players to see if we're all there. I count four and wonder who's missing, and it takes me a few moments to realise I've failed to count myself. The frightening thing was that the corridor did genuinely feel empty, as if even I wasn't there. I would try the card in the door one more time before going to report the fault. I shoved it into the slot, which pushed the door open half an inch with an audible click of the mechanism. I wondered if we'd left the door unlocked and what valuables might have been at risk. Then I heard the voice again, louder this time. It was coming from inside the room.

Moving Out

I don't know what she told her friends about her reasons for moving out, but I wasn't convinced it was just because of the new job. It was based on the east coast, seventy miles away. She could hardly commute, could she, her look seemed to say.

But did she really have to shift *all* her stuff and *buy* a flat rather than rent somewhere?

I thought we'd got on okay in my flat; it seemed to work fine. There was no indication that she tired of my frequent games and traps, which were never anything more than elaborate jokes. Sometimes, for fun, I used to try and frighten her, tense my muscles and affix an expression to my face, then move slowly towards her. She'd return the stare as long as she could, then fear crept into her eyes and I had to laugh to break the spell.

"Did I really frighten you?"

"Yes," she said, hurt.

"I'm sorry." I showed concern and concealed my pleasure. It was only a game.

She took everything. Her collection of masks left an empty wall in the bedroom, stubbled with nails. The bathroom shelf was suddenly made bare; forgotten tubs of moisturising cream and rolled-up tubes of toothpaste—even these things were taken. I saw her cast a mournful eye over my tailor's dummy.

"When I get my own place," she had once said, "will you give me this?"

She often asked. I didn't know why it was so important to her; she could have picked one up in any junk shop. I saw her from the kitchen one day, when she hadn't heard me come in from outside. She was kneeling at the mannequin's castors and clinging to its waist. Crying her eyes out.

I still didn't understand its significance.

She moved on a Saturday. I went along to help. Her new job came with a car, an estate, which was good because she would never have squeezed everything into my Mini.

I was ignored when I offered to drive. I knew what she'd say if she bothered to answer: I wasn't insured because we weren't married.

She didn't even give me chance to climb in next to her, before moving swiftly away from the kerb, spinning her wheels through a gutter full of litter.

I looked at the features of the Mini as I approached it. The radiator grille—the car's mouth—had been buckled for a couple of weeks, and one of the eyes had a smashed lens. I had to wrench the door open. The engine wheezed into life and I moved off. The front offside wheel scraped against the wheel arch, but a bald tyre was a small sacrifice. I'd said I'd help her move, and help her I would, with or without her cooperation.

I had my work cut out keeping up with her. She darted and surged, switching lanes in her haste as if there was no one else on the road. I had to rely on steady progress, the weight of the boxes in the back of her car and the re-tuning I'd had done two months earlier.

Her block of flats had a lift. If there hadn't been so many heavy boxes and bags to carry, she would have climbed the stairs, despite her flat being on the sixth floor. She had always hated lifts.

It wasn't just the discomfort of being crammed into what was basically a large tin, with a number of strangers; nor was it the embarrassment of awkward silences and accidentally crossed stares. Lifts terrified her.

Which offered me endless opportunities whenever we went anywhere and had to use a lift.

I only had to stand there, glaze my eyes over and turn slowly towards her, and she would panic.

"No, Nick! No!"

She once bolted out of a lift in a multi-storey carpark and ran straight into an old Vauxhall. She might have got away with a few bruises, had the car been stationary.

Some months later, one afternoon when she had gone out for a walk to help build up her strength, I rigged up a dummy out of some of my clothes, which I found in the wardrobe, and had it hanging in a noose from the kitchen doorway by the time she got back.

The relapse set her back about three months.

I regretted doing it but, as I explained, it was only a joke.

It always puzzled me why she liked masks when she was so easily frightened by faces.

"A mask is only a mask," she said. "It's not ambiguous. There's nothing behind it."

But in order to frighten her, I always had to start off by masking my features.

"There's nothing but wall behind my masks," she'd explained.

"Why do you like them so much?" I demanded.

"People used to believe that traumatic events that had not yet taken place could send back echoes from the future," she explained. "These echoes would sometimes register in masks."

"Like a satellite dish?" I quipped.

She gave me a black look.

"Why don't they show up in faces?" I asked.

"Because we block them. A mask can't. That's why you scare me when you fix your face like a mask. Sometimes the echoes are like the real thing."

❀

I stared at her now from the corner of the lift in her new home, but she looked no more distressed than she had when I'd snatched glances in her mirror during the drive up. Now it was her turn to wear a mask, the mask of tragedy. Yes, it would hurt, but she had to make the break. That kind of thing. Stony-faced resolve, with just the occasional glimpse of what looked like terror animating her glass eyes. She only had to say, if she didn't want me there.

But not a word was uttered. In fact, I couldn't recall the last time she had addressed me at all. I was blurring reality and imagination, not sure afterwards if she had said something or if I had imagined it from the look on her face.

The flat was on two floors. Not bad for the price and with a sweeping view of the sea front and port. At night the lights on the promenade would be pretty.

The staircase leading to the upper rooms was situated in the middle of the flat between the kitchen and the living room. You could walk right around the enclosed staircase, through the kitchen, the hallway and the living room. Actually under the stairs there was a cupboard, at its tallest about as tall as me.

I was able to follow her around from room to room and remain unseen. I tailed her just close enough to let her know I was there. She stopped and looked round, eyes flashing with anger and fear, but I was always just out of sight.

Later, after a light meal, I tried to talk to her. As if *I'd* done anything to upset *her*. "What's wrong?" I asked her.

She didn't feel like talking.

She slumped in a chair in front of the French windows. The curtains were closed, which meant she couldn't see the view. I pulled them back for her. It was dark now. The lights *were* pretty.

But with a snort she'd jumped up and quit the room as soon as I opened the curtain.

Anyone can take a hint, but it's somehow nicer to sit down and talk things out.

She clung to the edge of the sink, her face white as enamel.

"I'll make a drink," I suggested.

Thrusting out an arm she opened the fridge door and bent down to get the milk out. She started when she saw the car keys next to the butter. I'd put them there just after we'd arrived.

"What's the matter?" I pleaded.

I'd often hidden her things in the fridge at my flat, as a joke, her reaction never more than a laugh or a groan.

She slammed the fridge door, ignoring me, and ran upstairs, where she shut herself in her bedroom.

I took the keys out of the fridge and put them quietly down on the table, then sat down and thought about what might happen next. The simplest would be for me just to go. Would that be seen as giving in or a dignified withdrawal? Two of her Malaysian leather masks gazed unresponsively down at me from the wall above the portable television.

I became aware of a murmur of conversation through the ceiling. I stood up and craned my neck. Although the actual words were indistinguishable, I could tell it was her voice, and unanswered.

I walked quietly down the hall to the telephone extension. Hoping she wouldn't hear the click, I lifted the receiver to my ear.

" . . . Mini was his."

I frowned. What were they talking about?

" . . . but the things that are happening here, I'm terrified. I feel like I'm going mad or something. I keep hearing this terrible squealing."

I dropped the phone and rubbed my forehead, which was prickling with perspiration.

I couldn't decide what was the best thing to do, given her state of mind. But since my presence was obviously not helping, I decided to call it a day.

Closing the front door quietly behind me, I stepped into early morning darkness and thick fog. The car was some minutes' walk away. The plastic-covered seat was cold and sweating, the windscreen obscured inside and out. I proceeded, hunched over the wheel, the choke full out, wiping the condensation away with tissues and the fog with protesting wipers. The headlamps pushed into the fog, illuminating nothing but clouds of billowing moisture. The full beam was less help.

More by chance than navigation I found the dual carriageway and caught up with a set of red lights, which, when I narrowed the gap to eighteen inches, I could see belonged to a large container lorry.

In order to continue to enjoy the false security of the lorry's slipstream, I was obliged to accelerate to sixty miles per hour. I could scarcely credit the drivers who from time to time overtook me in the outside lane. My knees had liquified in the fear that I would fail to register the lorry's brake lights, should they come on.

Because of the unshrinking blanket of fog, I never saw the sign warning of roads merging and so remained ignorant of the danger until six lanes of traffic suddenly tried to squeeze into three.

Given the appalling visibility and the speed at which the influx of traffic was travelling (coming from the west, where the fog would be thinner), there were bound to be some casualties.

A USAF Jeep shunted me into the lorry I'd been sheltering behind, and an Audi overtaking on the outside caught my wing.

Then, dimly, I began to understand what she had meant about the echoes. Sometimes, she had said, the echoes are like the real thing.

❋

I only stayed long enough to pick up the tailor's dummy.

It would function as a present and as a surprise. Hopefully, she would have calmed down overnight and was probably already indulging herself in contrition.

Driving back up with the dummy lying silently on the back seat, I saw its bulk whenever I checked the rear-view mirror. Was it not too silent and bland? It needed a mask.

Also in the mirror I saw the mask I would give it.

The car coughed and clanked, but somehow made it.

She was out, at work, as I'd anticipated.

I went to the cupboard under the stairs. Three boxes sat in a corner and a couple of coats hung on hooks. The dummy, with its mask, was the same height as me.

Patiently I awaited the end of the working day.

I heard the key in the front door, the shuffle of letters, the tap of an executive briefcase on kitchen linoleum.

Footsteps. A yawn. More steps.

She pulled open the door.

A tremor went through her body; she stepped back; her mouth fell open but any sound was choked in her throat.

All apologies, I slid forward towards her, castors squealing.

"No, Nick! No!" she managed to say.

Jayne Anne Phillips

I'm in Amsterdam to promote my novel about doppelgängers. Checking into my hotel, I see Jayne Anne Phillips, the American novelist and short story writer, standing at the far end of the counter. I recognise her immediately because I saw her only last weekend at the '90s Fictions conference at the University of Sussex, where she said something about writing that I thought was interesting and wrote down in my notebook. The weird thing is she's looking at me too, also in apparent recognition. I say this is weird because in Brighton Jayne Anne Phillips was on the panel, appearing as an honoured guest, whereas I was a mere delegate. I sat near the back, didn't even raise my hand to ask a question. I can't believe I distinguised myself at all from those around me. Yet now we say hello, a little nervously, almost as if meeting an old friend with whom you are no longer sure of your standing, then the clerk hands her her key and she makes to go. We say goodbye, myself with the strange feeling that I may see her again.

When I get up to my room I throw open the windows, slightly disappointed that I have to crane my neck to see even part of a canal. But, with that excitement peculiar to the guest who enters his hotel room for the first time, I realise I had merely gone straight to the nearest window, seeing none other. Taking a step back, I now see that there is another window, albeit curtained, in the adjacent wall. I sweep the curtain aside and open a magnificent double window on to Herengracht. Gracht, the Dutch word for canal, is pronounced with a guttural H sound rather than a hard G, but I didn't know that on this my first visit to Amsterdam.

The telephone rings while I am unpacking my sponge bag and admiring my reflection in the bathroom mirror's flattering light. I walk back into the other room and answer the phone.

"It's me." A woman's voice. American.

"Hi," I say, uncertain how better to respond.

"You want to meet up?"

"Sure." Well, why not?

Without once using my name, she suggests a time and a place and rings off.

I enter a brown bar a little way down Herengracht and spot her sitting at a table by the full-length window. It looks as if she's having a drink with her twin sister, one of them sitting inside the bar, the other on the terrace overlooking the canal.

"Hi," she says in a surprised kind of way as if she'd been expecting somebody else.

"Can I get you a drink?"

"They come and serve you."

"Of course they do."

I sit down.

"I loved *Black Tickets*," I say. "They all started as dreams, didn't they?"

"I can't remember if they started as dreams and became real, or the other way around."

She can't settle, and is checking out everyone who enters the bar.

"Are you waiting for somebody?" I ask.

"As a matter of fact," she says, looking at me, "I was expecting somebody else. I was expecting Nicholas Royle, the author of *Telepathy and Literature* and books on Derrida. He teaches at Sussex, where the '90s Fictions conference took place."

"Well, actually," I say, "he doesn't teach there yet. He's still at Stirling."

We sit there for an hour, drinking, looking round at the other people in the bar, not talking much, although I remind her of the thing she said at Sussex that I had found interesting enough to write down.

"You said that writing is a kind of asbestos suit," I say.

She responds only with a weak smile.

We're still sitting there late into the evening and through the night. The following morning we still have not moved. Around about the end of the third day, she has begun to shade into transparency, and by sunrise on day four she has completely faded away. I remain sitting at the table for another hour before rising slowly to my feet and leaving the bar.

The Family Room

Have you ever sat in a parked car in a storm, counting the seconds between lightning flashes as bright as mercury and the timpani roll of thunder, while condensation slowly claims the windows? There's an almost-completed crossword on the empty seat beside you, but your concentration has gone, so you look for the half-seen reflection of car headlamps in your rear-view mirror and in the fish-eye lenses of individual raindrops as they trickle down the window.

There's silence from the back seat where your little girl, three last June, has fallen asleep.

The play of light creates a theatre of illusion: you keep thinking there's a break in the storm on the left side of the car. A bright patch of sky that isn't. A doorway out of reality.

Later, when you enter the pub, he's the first person you see. Alone at a table, a drink in front of him, he lifts his head but looks past you. He's got ten years on you and seems worn out, but otherwise it's like looking in the mirror. Perhaps for this reason, you take your drink over to his table and ask him if he minds if you join him.

He gestures at the empty chair and you take the weight off, taste your beer, forgetting to lick the froth from your upper lip.

"Rough night."

"Yes. I thought storms were supposed to pass overhead. This one's overstayed its welcome."

"It's here for the duration."

As the other man stares into his drink, you examine his face. Heather-hued shadows have been smudged in beneath his eyes. There are lines taut as kite strings across his brow, frown lines above the bridge of the nose that are as dark and forbidding as prison bars. His eyes are grey as the November skies over Northumberland.

The walls of the pub are partly hung with pictures—black and white photographs of the pub snowbound in the severe winter of 1963—and partly mirrored. Not in an '80s disco way; more like a Dublin snug with dark wood, bevelled glass.

"Have you ever been in a position where you don't know what to do?" the man asks you. "And yet you know you have to decide. Make a split-second decision. It's a matter of life and death, you might say."

Your judgment is beginning to look unsound. Having elected to sit with the pub bore, you now find yourself in a position where *you* are faced with a choice. Move on and give offence, or stay and risk death by a thousand clichés.

You shrug, half-smile, raise your glass. You're remembering sitting in the car, watching the raindrops roll down the windows. Each one seemed to contain the image of an approaching vehicle, until you actually looked directly at them and the lights vanished. The world seen not in a grain of sand but in a raindrop, and not so much seen as glimpsed—and then gone. The raindrop bumps over the rubber flange at the base of the window, slides down the car door and awaits its turn to drip off the bodywork altogether and land in the puddle that's forming beside the car.

"Do you see that fire?" the man asks you. "It never goes out. It would be nice that, wouldn't it? If the fire never went out?"

"What fire?"

"The fire inside you, you know."

The man was drunk, rambling.

"I mean what fire that never goes out? Where?"

"Over there."

The man points across to the right side of the bar where, in an enormous hearth partially obscured by a wooden pillar festooned with horse brasses, a few logs smoulder. From time to time, flames suddenly appear, shooting up the chimney, then vanish with as little warning.

"Why?" you ask.

"A hundred and twenty years ago, this pub was across the road. I mean there was a pub across the road and there wasn't one here. And it burned down, killing I don't know how many people. Middle of the night. The landlord survived, and, using the embers from the charred remains, lit a fire in the hearth of the building across the road—this building. It's never been allowed to go out since. So the landlord told me, anyway." The man raises his glass. "Not the same one, obviously."

"No."

"Plus, it gets very cold round here at this time of year."

"Yeah."

Now that you know about the fire, you become aware of tiny reflections of its occasional flames momentarily burnishing the wine glasses hanging upside down from their shelf behind the bar. It seems to you also that another, different light flares up now and then on the opposite side of the room. You never see it directly, but catch it in some of the room's many reflective surfaces.

You get up to go to the bar, noting your companion's readiness for a refill as you go. Somehow he seems to have kept pace with you. On your way to the bar, two little blonde-haired children cross your path, and you pause to let them go, a rock suddenly lodged in your throat. They disappear behind a pillar and you proceed to the bar, returning with a round of drinks to find the other man gone. You sit down, defeated, baffled. You'd just decided to persevere with the guy and now he's gone. You stand up, look around, glance in one of the mirrors and there you spot him. He's back, sitting down now. Accepting his drink without a word. Long, gulping swallow. Beer as thirst-quencher. Where's the fire?

"What's over there?" you ask him, indicating the other side of the room away from the hearth.

"That's the family room," he says and stares over your shoulder, his eyes red-rimmed, haunted.

His glass is empty again. An unacceptable state of affairs. He visits the bar, comes back with a tray: two pints and a Scotch each. Doubles. He hands you one. Won't drink his until your own is at your lips. Knock them back together. Beer to take the taste away—put out the whisky fire. He leans closer. So do you. Alcohol fumes mingle.

You wish you'd stayed in the car like before. Freya's blonde curls visible in the rear-view mirror. Unfinished crossword. Fifteen down: Crash street a measure above logo (4,8). Final clue.

"What was I supposed to do?" He half-stands, grabs your lapels and pulls you towards him. Your eyes swivel, looking for assistance. No one is taking any notice. Eyes cast down into drinks or lost in the fire. The landlord is wearing out his tea-towel polishing glasses that have already been polished. Outside, the dusk has turned swiftly to night and the storm is blowing itself out over the moors. You picture your car in the lay-by, dented front grille, Freya still strapped in her seat.

"What was I supposed to do? What would *you* do?" The man's whisper penetrates like a scream. "I'm driving along. I look behind for an *instant*, less than a second. Checking she's okay, you know? Making sure that she's *still there*. Have you never done that? And she smiles at me. It's like a light being switched on. The sun coming up. There's nothing more beautiful, you know? Have you got kids?"

You nod.

"Then you know."

He falters, seems unable to continue. You make a move to disentangle yourself.

"I look back at the road ahead," he says, strengthening his grip on your coat, "and as I do so my brain catches up with my eye and I develop the snapshot I've just taken of my little girl in her car seat. The print comes back from the lab in the time it takes me to refocus my eye on the road ahead and it shows me that she's undone her safety belt. It's not the first time, but usually you have time to do something about it. Roll into the side of the road, lean round, do it up, issue the standard reprimand. Only this time, this time I've looked back through the windscreen at the road ahead and I see I'm approaching a crossing. There are some people on the crossing. Two little girls and their mother. One of the little girls, baby blonde, is dawdling. Her darker sister is already a yard ahead and her mother is looking back, repeating a previous instruction that she keep up, especially on the road. And then she sees me coming, the mother, she sees my car and her face looks like *it's* the one that's going to get hit, like it's already *been* hit. It's ironed flat, eyes like dinner plates, mouth opening to scream.

"What do I do? Do I slam on the brakes to save the child on the crossing, knowing that to do so will catapult my own daughter out of her seat, over the top of the empty front passenger seat, head first into the windscreen? Or do I keep going, lifting my foot off the gas, as if that will make any difference, but not touching the brake pedal, and hit the little girl dawdling on the crossing with the kind of force that will lift her off the ground, a bag of broken bones, and fling her thirty yards down the road to land on her head? What do I do? What would *you* do? This goes through my mind like two-plus-two through the brain of a supercomputer. Faster. I still have time to act. Which child do I kill? My own or that of the woman watching?"

"It's an impossible choice," you say.

"You think so?" says the man, his hands falling away as he slumps back down in his seat.

Raised voices distract you. The landlord is shouting at the two little girls you saw earlier to get away from the fire. Giggling, they scamper away behind a pillar.

"Kids," mutters the landlord as he snaps his tea-towel over his shoulder and comes out from behind the bar. "That's what the family room's for. So customers can drink in peace and quiet."

By the time he reaches the hearth, the girls have disappeared to another part of the bar.

You look at your drinking buddy. He looks beaten, defeated, like a fighter on the ropes.

"What did you decide?" you ask him.

"What?" He looks up at you with hollow eyes. "I didn't. I didn't decide. I couldn't."

You can hardly bear to hold his stare.

"What happened?" you ask.

"You know what happened."

The landlord is creating again. "One hundred and twenty years," he's grumbling in his wounded, resentful voice to anyone who'll listen, "More than a century that fire was burning. Look at it now."

To illustrate his point, he plunges a hand into the ashes and retrieves it undamaged.

"Bloody kids."

You look back across the table at your drinking partner, who is still staring intently at you.

You break the spell by getting up and walking away. The fire is out. The landlord is scowling behind his counter, pulling his tea-towel endlessly though his rough hands. You walk towards the lights of the family room.

The two little blonde girls—one with straight hair, the other a tumble of curls—are bent over one of the tables, their faces hidden. The family room is over-lit, fluorescent tubes. The tables are Formica-topped, modern, with sticky rings from ketchup bottles, fizzy drinks. The character of the main bar is absent here. Cheap prints badly framed on the wall. This is an afterthought, a grudge-extension, provided out of meanness, decorated with spite.

When the two little girls hear you approaching, they turn round to face you. The harsh lighting suddenly seems particularly unforgiving.

Cuckoo

Swift stepped down from the train in the dark suit that his ex-wife, Maggie, had often joked was his writer's outfit, but really, what else could he wear? He waited on the platform for a moment while the other travellers headed towards the exit. The train departed and was soon no more than a dot in the distance. Swift took off his glasses and cleaned them using the duster he kept neatly folded in his notebook. Once he felt the stillness of the empty platform settling around him, he lifted his bag on to his shoulder.

On his way out of the station, he stopped by a piece of public art: a poem printed on a board fixed to the wall. It was a poem about the large station clock that was suspended above the platform. Swift had always maintained that as a novelist he was unqualified to judge poetry, but he silently congratulated the poet for her description of the clock's "poker face and sorrowful hands". In 1978, he read, the great clock's mechanical workings had been replaced by an electrical mechanism, which had evidently been a poor and inadequate substitute.

> *They say it was the water getting in*
> *That stopped it dead at half past three*
> *But I say it had had enough*
> *Of that cuckoo nesting deep within*

He walked on, allowing himself no more than a glance at the tearooms where a celebrated film had once been shot.

Leaving the station, he looked at his watch. There was time before the reading, not only to visit the bookshop, but to walk around the town. He had deliberately caught an early train. As he crossed the small car park, a woman passed him from left to right. He did a double take. The chestnut bob, the pale skin at the back of the neck. The way she held her head slightly downturned, even the hurried walk, leaning forward. The woman got into a car, started its engine and drove directly out of the car park.

It wasn't her, but it looked like her.

It couldn't have been her.

He, too, left the car park and looked both ways. He could walk left over the railway bridge and out into open countryside, or right, up the slight incline towards the crossroads at the centre of the town. That way lay the venue for the reading, but there was plenty of time.

Faint screams reached his ears, prompting him to raise his pointed chin. Sickle-shaped birds scratched at the cornflower-blue sky. Swifts, *Apus apus*, harbingers of summer. (They were early this year, as they had been the year before and the year before that.) Even when associated with summer, "harbinger" carried a brooding undertone. Had he ever used the word, Swift wondered? He had read recently that the swift population was declining because of a shortage of nesting sites. Almost invariably they nested in old buildings, in the eaves or in holes in the brickwork, and as more and more of these were fixed up or barred with pigeon netting, so the swift was rendered homeless.

Not that they spent that much time in their nests. The swift lived more of its life on the wing than any other bird—feeding, drinking, mating, even sleeping during flight. But with no nesting sites there would be no young and with no young eventually there would be no birds at all.

Swift had made it his business to find out about the swift.

The legs of the swift were very short, little used, almost vestigial. A grounded bird would often find itself marooned and never fly again.

Their piercing cries were supposed to symbolise the screaming of lost souls.

He walked up the hill, where a toyshop caught his eye. Among the brightly coloured boxes of board games and packs of cards was a display of model animals that made his breath catch in his throat. These were not the cheaply made, roughly moulded plastic models he had got used to seeing over the years whenever he had looked in a toyshop window or taken a shortcut across the toy floor of a department store—made in the Far East, with more of an eye to profit than for detail. These, instead, were the models he had played with as a boy. The same make. He recognised the tiny painted hooves of the farmyard goat, the resplendent mane of the roaring lion, the erect gorilla with its fists in the air.

Swift had always liked small towns. He had always thought the phrase "small-town mentality" unfair to small towns with their family-run shops and their pavements and squares that were gathering places for friends and neighbours. He lived in the city, where rest was impossible. There was always a deadline to meet, a reading to get to, a book to finish, the next one to start.

Swift's feet never touched the ground.

Next door to the toyshop, a window filled with computers and printers and modems and scanners, and at the heart of this display of the very latest hardware a big beautiful old typewriter. Swift wondered if the tug of familiarity was just a tiny bit specific. The machine reminded him of the one on which he had composed his first novel, the one in which he had written about Agnes.

He remembered the woman in the car park, the vulnerability of the back of her neck. Just like Agnes, whom he had known before Maggie.

There was still time, but he had to make sure he didn't miss the bookshop. His research had told him there was a second-hand bookshop with a decent stock and a good reputation. Swift loved books. He loved reading them, he loved collecting them, he loved sitting on the floor late at night taking them from his shelves at random to gaze at the cover and run his fingers over the title page. Towards the end of his marriage, he had had to start sneaking books into the house.

You'll never read all of these, she'd said.

That wasn't the point, he'd replied.

Swift wondered if Terrence loved books—Terrence, who had cuckolded Swift—if he read books, if he sat on the floor late at night surrounded by uniform editions of an author's works while the clocks ticked and Maggie breathed slowly in her sleep.

The bookshop was located by the crossroads, which he could now see up ahead where the traffic lights were on red. The bookshop was soon revealed on the other side of the road. The door closed behind him with the tinkle of a bell. Around him were racks of cards and gift books. A sign pointed upstairs. Swift was glad of the handrail as he climbed.

He went where he always went, to paperback fiction. Swift wasn't a serious collector; he collected for pleasure. His eyes grazed the spines, slowing down as he experienced joyous moments of recognition. There was a book he owned. There was another. And another and another and another. This was not unusual; Swift owned a great many books. But perhaps it was unusual that in this grazing he had yet to spot a title that was *not* among his collection. He slowed down and read spine after spine, trailing his finger to aid concentration. He read spine after spine after spine. On this shelf, on this wall, he had them all. He moved to the next wall, authors from H to M. At eye-level were the Ks. Kavan, Kenworthy, Kilworth, Knowles, Kureishi. He had them all. It wasn't just that he owned books by all these authors; he owned these very titles. He started to look for books he didn't have. He searched among Kavan's titles for *The Parson*. They didn't have it. Neither did he.

It was coincidence. He moved across to the shelves on the facing wall. Towards the end of the alphabet. Here too there was nothing he didn't already have. He darted around, dipping in and out of letters, looking for specific authors, for particular types of novel. The Angry Young Men: he had them all, all the ones they had. Experimental novelists: the same ones were here as were on his own shelves at home. He began looking for books from obscure presses, American publishers. Elastic Press, Chronicle Books, Prime Books, Red Hen Press. All present, but only the ones he owned. He looked for rare books. He looked for a book he had once owned and let go and then spent twenty-five years searching for so that he could read it again. He had found it. It, too, was here.

Swift backed out of the room, as if afraid its contents might follow him out, and the handrail took his weight as he descended the staircase. The bell tinkled as he opened the door, but it was a hollow tinkle. He stepped outside. The air was comfortably warm. The distant screams of swifts could still be heard and against them, coming from somewhere beyond the railway station, the unmistakeable springtime call of the male cuckoo, *Cuculus canorus*.

Three uniformed policemen passed by on the opposite side of the road, one of them controlling a black-and-white spaniel by means of a lead and harness with fluorescent trim.

Swift leaned back against the brick wall of the bookshop and took a handkerchief from his pocket with which he wiped his eyes. Then he blew his nose, with a trumpeting flourish. He didn't know if he had ever forgiven Maggie, because she had never asked for his forgiveness. He had always felt slightly lost, since she had left. Like a lost soul, restless.

He started walking back towards the railway station. He had come to regard *it*, rather than the crossroads, as the centre point, or pivot, of the town, despite the fact it clearly occupied—or possibly created—a marginal, liminal sector in which it, a taxi firm, a pub and a fast-food outlet were the only signs of human activity.

As Swift walked down the incline, he heard loud music approaching at speed. He turned around, frowning at a trapped nerve in his back, to see a souped-up red saloon car decelerating fast as it came level with the bookshop. The driver turned down the volume on his sound system almost to zero as he passed Swift, who was surprised to see him doff his white baseball cap while rolling the car slowly down the hill.

The car had disappeared by the time Swift realised the driver's face had been familiar, but, like a face seen in a dream, it was then impossible to place.

He walked past the car park and started to climb the low bridge over the railway. At the top he stopped and rested his arms on the parapet, from where he could enjoy a view of the station. The policemen who had passed him earlier seemed to be performing a security check of the platforms and railway buildings. The spaniel was still on its lead and was being encouraged to sniff at drains, manhole covers and those little trapdoors that conceal the interior workings of lampposts. Swift wondered what might be going on. There was a gathering of important political leaders taking place in the capital, but that was more than wo hundred miles away. Could one of them be coming up here at the conclusion of the conference? It seemed unlikely.

Cuck-oo, cuck-oo, cuck-oo.

Swift looked to the west. There was a stand of trees a quarter of a mile away. Then more open land and a wood beyond. Everyone has heard a cuckoo—and its parasitic behaviour is general knowledge—yet relatively few have ever seen one.

Turning to look in the other direction, towards the town, Swift saw that beyond it lay a hill with a church or some kind of monument at its summit. A graveyard perhaps. A crown of trees.

The policemen, meanwhile, had reached the tearooms on the middle platform. Swift wondered if they would have to go inside. He glimpsed a stutter of images from the well-known film that had been shot there. Clipped voices, shades of grey. Cauliflower clouds of soot-flecked steam. Baggy suit trousers, trenchcoat and trilby. Pillbox hat. Tightly fitted skirt. How much he recalled and how much was invention, he couldn't say. But he remembered the music, a piano concerto, richly romantic, full of yearning. Forced separation. Tears, heaving bosoms.

In the end, she—the conflicted heroine at the apex of the film's relationship triangle—had abandoned her lover and stuck by her husband. *You've been a long way away.* Yes. *Thank you for coming back to me.*

Maggie, too, had been a long way away – but had not come back to him.

Cuck-oo, cuck-oo.

Swift had seen the film many times. Before, during and after the break-up of his marriage. Mainly after. In the film, the lover had been terribly, terribly British. Took it on the chin. Terrence hadn't needed to. Swift remembered the day he had come home to find Terrence in their home, standing there with Maggie, and she had attempted to laugh it off as nothing serious, tossing her tight auburn curls. Terrence had stood there in the centre of their living room, with his open-neck shirt and his sports jacket, surrounded by Swift's bookshelves. Smoking some kind of bitter-smelling cigarette. This was their home, Swift remembered thinking, their nest.

Some excuse had been made and Terrence had departed, but Maggie had left soon afterwards and, apart from at his father's funeral, when she had hovered at a distance, Swift had never seen her again.

Swift walked back down the town side of the railway bridge and crossed the car park to re-enter the station. He passed under the tracks by means of the pedestrian tunnel and caught up with the policemen by the site of the poem he had read on his arrival. He politely asked what was going on and one of the officers told him a VIP was expected. He asked them who it was. The policeman exchanged a glance with one of his colleagues, then smiled grimly, adding that he wasn't at liberty to say.

Swift looked at the great station clock as he turned to go. The reading was shortly due to begin. He passed beneath the tracks and traversed the car park. He misjudged the height of the curb and tripped, his glasses falling off his nose and landing with a sharp snap on the pavement. With difficulty he bent to pick them up. One lens was cracked in two places. He had always preferred glass lenses because they didn't scratch. They broke instead.

He folded the glasses away into his jacket pocket and walked back towards the centre of the town. He felt smaller and everything around him seemed both dangerously close and yet further away. People loomed as they passed him, indistinct yet full of a threatening familiarity. When he reached the crossroads, he took the broken glasses from his pocket and put them on. Straight on, the road continued to climb the hill, past a guest house and on towards the church or monument he had seen from the railway bridge. He felt an attraction, but he knew it was time for his reading. He had never missed a reading, never left a venue while there was still someone waiting to get a book signed.

So he turned right, fumbling his glasses back into his pocket, and half-guessed, half-felt his way past the pub he had been told was there, until he reached the right building. A flight of steps led upwards. He climbed them with difficulty, passing a man in a sports jacket standing on the top step smoking a cigarette.

Once inside, Swift removed his glasses from his pocket and put them on. Right away he could see he had entered via the wrong door. The room was full and the table containing copies of his books was at the far end of the room. Two women stood between the table and another doorway, clearly the one through which he ought to have arrived. While deciding what he should do, he allowed his gaze to settle on the audience.

The room was full, as if the whole town had turned out to hear him read, as if *he* were the VIP whose arrival had been expected.

A ridiculous idea, unless the town were not an ordinary town.

He looked from one face to the next—even in three-quarter profile they could easily be made out—and from one row to the next. His gaze scanned the whole room. Row after row. Face after face after familiar face.

In the front row, by an empty seat, the back of a head, tight shoulder-length curls, still the same shade of auburn with perhaps a little help.

He removed his broken glasses as he turned back to the doorway by which he had come in, his breaths laboured.

As he exited the building, he passed someone coming back in trailing a cloud of pungent cigarette smoke. A bitter, heady aroma.

Swift stumbled as he negotiated the steps, but righted himself. Speed was important, he sensed, in case he should be followed.

At the crossroads and traffic lights, he turned right, crossing the road, and started making his slow, painful way up the hill. Away from the town, away from the railway station. As he climbed, he saw them all again, row upon row upon row.

He wanted to stop, needed a rest, but somehow he kept going, dragging his feet up the hill. He pictured the church, the graveyard, the crown of trees. At the top he would rest. In peace.

Above him in the darkening sky, the swifts had fallen silent, but still those tiny black sickles continued to sweep back and forth.

Extract from "Stations of the Clock" by Lynne Alexander.

This Video Does Not Exist

I wake up two minutes before the alarm is due to go off. I cancel the alarm and lie still for a few moments, trying to remember my dreams, with limited success. All I can sense is a vague feeling of loss or nostalgia. In a moment my wife will stir and I will climb out of bed and open the curtains.

"The Manchester skies are grey," I say as I look outside. How many times have I said these words upon opening the curtains? When does a running joke become an annoying habit? I suspect I will not find out until one day, when, instead of sleepily murmuring some benign response, my wife will retort, "We made the decision *together* to leave London. You know that as well as I do," or "It's been three years now. Can you not leave it alone?"

I forestall the possibility of this happening today by asking her, "Would you like some tea?"

"Yes, please," says a voice from under the duvet.

I leave the bedroom. I enter the bathroom and open the window blind. The Manchester skies are grey at the rear of the house as well. I wonder what the weather is like in London. I imagine a version of myself opening curtains and blinds in London right now and reporting to a version of my wife that the London skies are blue. I feel certain that if I check the weather online it will be two degrees cooler in Manchester than in London.

I use the toilet, then move to the sink. I lean on the edge of the washbasin, staring at the spotless white porcelain beneath my hands.

How many mornings have I done what I'm about to do? How many mornings have I raised my head to see the same reflection looking back at me? How many mornings have I thought that I am looking old, that I may be closer to the end of my life than its beginning?

This morning, however, is different.

This morning I do not look older, but I do look as if the end of my life is upon me.

The man in the mirror is wearing the same crumpled t-shirt that I am wearing, although the writing across the chest is back to front, as you would expect. The arms are the same—lightly tanned, freckled. The neck is the same slightly scrawny neck that makes me look my age in photographs. But above the neck—nothing. No tired eyes, lined forehead, stubbly cheeks. No vertical frown line above the bridge of the nose. Nothing.

I look at my neck, but I can't see the end of it. There is no stump. Neither a flat, cartoonish disc like the end of a ham, nor the scraggy, gory mess of a victim in a splatter movie. Instead, it is like a tall building, its top lost in the clouds. I just can't see it.

I raise my hands—I see them rise in the mirror—but there is nothing for them to alight on. No puffy skin beneath my eyes, no incipient jowls. I cannot feel the stubble on the top of my head, which I shaved only two days ago. The top of my head is not there. My head is not there.

The man in the mirror has no head.

I turn from the washbasin and look out of the window. The sky remains grey. I look back in the mirror. I still have no head. I step away, turn around, walk towards the door, then come back to the washbasin and look in the mirror

148

again. No change. With my fingers I try to feel where my neck ends, but I can't seem to gain purchase. Any sensation in my finger tips is weak. I don't know where or how my neck ends, but I know that it ends and that there is nothing above it.

I pause in the bathroom doorway. My wife is waiting for her tea. She will not wake fully until I bring it to her. I step out on to the carpeted landing. I can walk normally. I can see, even though I have no eyes to see with. I can hear birds singing in the trees at the front of the house. A slightly sour smell of bedding rises from my t-shirt as I head towards the stairs. I walk downstairs, my sense of balance unaffected. I enter the kitchen, fill the kettle and switch it on.

Every morning I start emptying the dishwasher while the kettle is boiling and complete the job while the tea is brewing. As I bend down to remove the cutlery basket, I ask myself if bending down feels any different. Sometimes I bend down too quickly and once I have straightened up again I feel light headed. This time, that doesn't happen.

I carry two cups of tea upstairs. I stand in front of the bedroom door as I remember approaching a road junction on my bike a day or two ago and not seeing a car that was coming towards me, because I was so intent on looking left and right. I saw it in time, but I had, for a few moments, been blind to it. I wonder if what I am experiencing now is a form of hysterical or selective blindness. I ask myself if I should place the cups of tea down on top of the bookcase on the landing and return to the mirror in the bathroom and have another look. But as I think this, I hear my wife getting out of bed and suddenly the bedroom door is open and she is standing in front of me.

"Oh," she says, giving a little jump. "You frightened me."

"Really?" I say.

"Yes, I didn't know you were there. Thank you," she says, taking one of the cups and moving past me to go to the bathroom. Did she actually look at me? I can't be sure.

I enter the bedroom and check in the full-length mirror my wife uses when she is getting dressed. There is no change. If I were more detached from the situation I would find it interesting. It would thrill me on a number of levels—aesthetic, visceral, intellectual. But it's hard to be detached.

My wife re-enters the bedroom and starts to get things out of her chest of drawers. She glances at me standing in front of the mirror and makes a humorous remark.

I ignore it and ask her, "Do I look tired to you?"

"Did you go to bed late?"

"Just look at me! Do I look tired to you?"

She turns and looks at me for a moment.

"There's no need to snap," she says. "You look neither tired nor not tired."

"Thanks," I say. "That's very helpful."

"Are you going to drink that?" she asks, lowering her eyes to the cup of tea I am still holding in my hand.

"Yes," I say. "No . . . I don't know."

I leave the bedroom with the cup of tea and pour it away down the sink in the bathroom.

"I'm going to have a shower," I shout.

"I'll be gone when you're done," my wife shouts back. "So I'll see you later."

"Okay. See you later."

I lock the bathroom door and look at myself in the mirror. No change.

I run the shower and wait until I hear the front door before switching it off. I return to the bedroom and start getting dressed, leaving my top half until last. I open my wardrobe and consider the separate piles of neatly folded t-shirts sorted by colour. I pick out a black one.

Downstairs I pull on my fluorescent jacket and zip it up. I open the cupboard where the rest of my cycling paraphernalia is kept and look at my helmet. I reach out and touch the cool plastic with a finger tip, but then withdraw my hand and close the cupboard door.

Cycling down our road I feel the wind on my face like pain in a phantom limb. I cut through the park, where dog-walkers take hold of their animals' collars at my approach and joggers carry water bottles shaped like bagels. Everything as normal, in other words. Exiting the park, I notice a woman waiting to cross the road; I nod to indicate she can go and she does, raising a hand in thanks.

I reach the university and find that someone has saved me the trouble of opening the door to the bike shelter. A colleague whose name I can never remember is struggling to get his bike past those nearest the door.

One of us comments on the inadequacy of the bike shelter's design and the other agrees. We lock up our bikes and leave and so enter the building at the same time. He presses the button for the lift and when it arrives and the doors slide open he gestures for me to go first. In the mirrored walls of the elevator I see a sequence of reflections of a headless man in a fluorescent jacket.

"Departmental meeting in half an hour," says my colleague.

"Yeah," I say. "I'm counting the minutes."

In the meeting, I sit next to Andy. Like me, Andy teaches film. I can see us reflected in the windows across the room.

"Andy," I say, "you'd tell me if I had, like, egg on my chin or something, right?"

Andy turns to look at me, leaning back as he does so. "What are you trying to say?"

"Do I look normal to you?"

"Define normal."

"Right," I say.

"I hope this doesn't go on for four hours like last time," he says. "I'm going to that London tomorrow and I've got a ton of marking to get done before then."

"Tell me about it. What you going to that London for?"

"Externals meeting at Birkbeck."

"Lucky you."

"Birkbeck?"

"London," I say. "I mean, Birkbeck as well, but, you know, just London."

The meeting proceeds along the usual lines. Every time we seem to have reached, if not a decision, then at least the end of the latest pointless discussion on a particular topic, one person, always the same person, will raise her hand and make a point that invariably starts with the words "I'm sorry, but . . . " and prompts further inconclusive debate, meaning that the end of the meeting is delayed by another ten or fifteen minutes. We are on the last item on the agenda—safety and environment—and a heated discussion about evacuation procedures for wheelchair users has just reached a sort of conclusion when a colleague—the same colleague—sticks her hand up and starts, "I'm sorry, but . . . " and I turn to Andy, who is already turning to me and drawing the blade of his right hand across his throat. The gesture makes me widen my eyes, but, if Andy notices, he fails to react.

After the meeting I sit in my office with a pile of dissertations on the desk in front of me. I open the top one and turn to the first page, read the opening paragraph and see that the writer has failed to make correct use of the semi-colon. I close the dissertation. There's a knock on the door. I look around, sit up straight in my chair, aware of a slight increase in my heart rate.

"Come in," I hear myself say.

The door opens to reveal a third-year undergraduate, Rebecca, whose dissertation I remember supervising.

"Hiya," she says. "I wanted to see you to talk about doing an MA."

"Come in," I say. "Sit down." I move the dissertations to one side of my desk. "I imagine yours is in this lot somewhere," I tell her.

She smiles.

"So you want to do an MA? That's great news."

"In London," she says.

"Oh."

"At Goldsmiths' or UCL or somewhere. I wanted to see if you thought that would be a good idea."

I look at her. She is one of those students my wife thought I would be tempted to have an affair with, or tempted to try to have an affair with: bright, attractive, a good critic, potentially susceptible to flattery from a widely published academic. She raises her eyebrows; the corners of her mouth turn up.

"No, I think it's a terrible idea," I say, watching her face fall, then leave it a couple of moments before adding: "I think you should do it here."

She laughs. "I really want to live in London," she says.

I look away at a line of DVDs standing between bookends on my desk. *Apocalypse Now*, *The Tenant*, *Eraserhead*, *Se7en*.

"Actually, I think it's a great idea," I say, turning back towards Rebecca. "I'll write you a reference. I did the same thing myself twenty-five years ago." As I say it I realise the figure is actually closer to thirty. "It was when I saw all these for the first time," I add, indicating the films on my desk. "Well, apart from *Se7en*."

"That's great. Thanks," she says, looking straight into my eyes.

"You're welcome."

There is a pause. I often fill such pauses, feeling it is unfair to expect students to do so, but on this occasion I say nothing.

"So," she says, finally, "do you think I'll get in?"

"To one of those courses? Oh yes. You can punctuate a sentence."

She laughs uncertainly, pauses and then says, "Is that it? I can punctuate a sentence?"

"You'd be surprised how unusual that makes you these days," I say. "But luckily that's not all. You're one of the good ones. You're one of the ones I come in for. One of the ones I get up in the morning for."

"Thank you," she says, "I think."

"Rebecca?" I say.

"Yes?"

"Do I look any different to you today?"

"Er."

"It's all right. You don't have to answer that." I lift my hand, instinct or habit making me want to run it over my shaved head. Instead, it hovers in mid-air.

Rebecca gets up. "Thanks again," she says.

"You're welcome. Good luck. Put me down for those references," I say as she opens the door and leaves my office.

I watch the corridor through the doorway, which she has left open. A couple of first-year students pass by. I turn again to the pile of dissertations on my desk and look through them for Rebecca's. I pull it out, turn to the first page and read the opening paragraph, then close it and write on the marksheet: 80%.

I get my stuff together, thread my arms into my fluorescent jacket and pause with my hand on the door handle. I look back. I return to my desk and go through the dissertations until I find the first one I'd been looking at, the one with the faulty punctuation. I write on the marksheet: 50%.

I cycle home, where I go straight upstairs and stand in front of the bathroom mirror. I try to focus on my neck. I want to examine the extremity. But every time I get close to doing so, I find my mind drifting from the specific task in hand to my more general preoccupation with the overall problem—or absence. I get a hand mirror and hold it behind me, picturing as I do so a well-known Magritte painting of a man viewed from behind looking into a mirror, not at the reflection of his face, but at the back of his own head. This is what I should see in the reflected hand mirror, the back of my head, but I don't. If anything, this confirmation that my head is missing when viewed from behind—as well as from in front—is even more dismaying than the original sight in the mirror that morning, perhaps because I am mimicking the view that others have of me from behind, without my knowledge, without my ability to be aware, without any self-consciousness. But, instead, I wonder if it should encourage me that other people—my wife, strangers in the street, my colleagues and students—see nothing wrong.

Or nothing different from normal.

I have wandered out of the bathroom and now find myself in the bedroom, standing at the window looking down into the street. A neighbour from a few doors down walks past with her dogs and looks up and waves. I wave back. She sees nothing amiss. Can she not see? Is it that she is not looking at me properly?

I realise that I ought to be reminded of a different Magritte painting, in which a dead woman lies on a red couch, her head and neck at an unnatural angle to her body, a white scarf obscuring the conjunction of neck and torso.

I take my phone out of my pocket and open the address book. I find the number for the local GP surgery and my finger hovers over the call button for a moment. I look out of the window, see my neighbour turning the corner at the end of the street with her dogs. I press the button. A couple of rings and then the recorded voice of the practice manager. I know the spiel: I press the appropriate key to get through to make an appointment.

The receptionist offers me an appointment in a week's time. I tell her I don't necessarily have to see my own doctor. I'll see one of the others. She says I can see one of the other doctors in three days' time. I tell her I need to see someone today. She asks if it is an urgent matter. I pause for a moment, then tell her, yes, it is. She asks if I can explain what the problem is. I remain silent for a few seconds, thinking. She says my name, asks if I am still there. I tell her I can't tell her what the problem is. It's personal. She says she understands and that I should come down to the surgery and they will fit me in as soon as they can.

I walk down the road and enter the surgery. I see the receptionist and then sit in the waiting room and watch a procession of people with heads on their shoulders getting called to see the doctor before I do. Finally, I hear my name. I get up and leave the waiting room. As I turn into the corridor that leads to the consulting rooms I catch sight of my reflection in a pane of reinforced glass in the door that leads to the stairs. There's the same empty space where my head should be and, I presume, used to be. Is it possible I never had a head, but only hallucinated it? What kind of question is that to be asking yourself as you knock on your GP's door and hear her invite you to enter?

"Good morning, doctor," I say. "How are you?"

"Very well, thank you," she says, meeting my gaze. "How are you?"

I think carefully about my response. "I'm not sure," I say finally. "I suppose I want you to tell me."

"Well," she says, "you requested an emergency appointment."

"Yes," I say.

The doctor looks at me. Her face betrays neither surprise nor dismay, nor the slightly indecent excitement a doctor might feel when presented with an unusual case.

"I feel," I say, "like something is missing."

The doctor smiles and frowns at the same time.

"From your . . . life?"

"Something is missing and I feel as if I can't carry on without it, and yet it's very hard to say what it is . . . what it is that's missing. Do you see?"

"Have you been feeling depressed?" she asks.

"More alarmed than depressed," I say.

"Have you been feeling anxious?"

I look at her, unsure how to respond.

"Panic attacks, uncontrollable distress?"

I look away from her towards the frosted glass of the window.

"Do you feel as if you are losing your grip?" she asks.

"I think I need to go," I say.

The smile has disappeared and now there is only a concerned frown.

"If you'd like to see someone . . . a referral?"

"I'm okay," I say, getting to my feet. "I'll be okay."

"Are you sure?"

"I'm fine."

"Make an appointment to see me in a week or two."

I thank her and leave. I walk back home without delay.

I stand in the hall. The house is silent. I'm thinking. I go into the kitchen and open the drawer where we keep the larger saucepans and the rice cooker. Then I close it again. I try the tall cupboards. I open all the eye-level cupboards and look quickly inside each one before closing them again. I open the fridge. Milk, wine, butter, cheese, salad stuff, yoghurts, a bowl containing leftover chilli that will inevitably be thrown away.

In the cellar I open the doors to all the cupboards. I look in the old plastic dustbin I store firewood in. The shelves—nothing that shouldn't be there, just jam jars containing screws and curtain hooks and Allen keys and brass hooks bought to go on the backs of doors that have never been fitted.

I climb the steps back to the hall. There are cupboards in the lounge containing LPs that have not been played in twenty years. The cushions on the settee conceal only biscuit crumbs, loose change and the TV remote control that has been missing for two days.

Upstairs I check the wardrobes and the airing cupboard. I pull down piles of bedding and towels and leave them in a heap on the bathroom floor. I rummage behind the hot water tank. I look around the landing. The linen basket contains nothing but a few pairs of socks and some under-wear. I take the stairs to the top floor and my study. The drawers of my filing cabinet are filled with hanging files overstuffed with papers and manuscripts and press cuttings. I look at the bookshelves. Books, DVDs, VHS tapes, copies of *Sight & Sound* going back fifteen years. There are no gaps on the shelves. There is nothing under my desk except my printer and a box I use as a foot-rest and lots of fluff and dust-furred wires and cables.

I go back down to the first floor. There's an empty wardrobe in the spare bedroom, but that's exactly what it is—empty. I carry a stool in from the bedroom and stand on it so I can see on top of the empty wardrobe, but all I see is empty space.

Slowly I walk downstairs. I open the front door and step outside. I approach the bins. The brown one, emptied re-cently, contains a couple of wine bottles and several tin cans; the blue bin is two-thirds filled with paper and cardboard; the green one is less than half-filled with grass cuttings and compostable bags of food waste; and the grey bin conceals a single bag of non-recyclable rubbish collected from various bins and baskets around the house. It has a drawstring neck and the plastic tape used to secure it has been tied in a knot.

I look up from the bin. The windows of the house across the street return a blank stare.

I reach into the grey bin and pull out the bag. I dump it on the drive and bend down to pick at the knot. It won't come, so I press my finger nails into the plastic at the top of the bag and tear it open. The bag is almost full. I plunge my hands into a mass of stained cotton wool balls, disintegrating toilet roll holders and spaghetti in tomato sauce that should have gone in the green bin. There are damp tissues and an empty blister pack of heavy-duty pain killers and a rolled-up ball of my wife's hair. Well, it's certainly not mine. I picture her standing at the sink, viewed through the half-open door, pulling the hair out of her brush and rolling it into a ball between her palms, looking up and seeing me watching her and then looking away to direct her right foot at the pedal bin.

I pick the bag up by its bottom corners and upend it over the drive. Its contents hit the asphalt in a large pile into which I delve, coming up empty handed.

As I'm shovelling the worst of the mess back into the bag, one of my neighbours walks past the end of the drive. She gives me a look similar to the one the doctor gave me.

My wife comes home.

"What's all that mess on the drive?" she asks.

"I was looking for something," I say. "I'll clean it up."

I pour her a glass of wine, which she takes through into the lounge, while I locate the dustpan and brush in the cupboard under the sink. I hear the television go on and a newsreader's voice saying something about the situation in Syria. Violence in Damascus. Calls to arm the rebels. I take the dustpan and brush outside and start clearing up the mess. When I come back in, I can hear a reporter on the news doing a piece to camera. I stow the dustpan and brush and go upstairs to put the towels away and anything else I've left lying around in my hunt through various cupboards and drawers.

As I come back downstairs and enter the lounge, I hear another news reporter saying, "The head was removed by police, who are conducting further enquiries."

"*What's that?*" I say, aware of the sharpness in my voice.

"Severed head found in a plastic bag in London," my wife says, before draining her wine glass. "Was that an especially small glass you gave me?" she asks.

"What?"

"It didn't last long."

"*What?*"

"That glass of wine."

"What about the head, the severed head on the news?"

"I don't know," she says. "I wasn't really paying attention. Someone found a severed head in a Sainsbury's bag."

"Where?"

"I don't know. London, somewhere."

"Did you see it?"

"The head?"

"Yes."

"Of course I didn't see it. They're not going to put a severed head on the six o'clock news, are they?"

"Where in London was it? They must have said."

"I daresay they did. I wasn't really listening. What difference does it make? A severed head is a severed head wherever it's found."

I grab the remote and press rewind. The details are that a man's severed head was discovered by a woman out walking her dog at ten past eight that morning on the Parkland Walk between Highgate and Finsbury Park. It was, as my wife had said, inside a supermarket carrier bag.

"I wonder if it was a bag-for-life?" my wife says.

On to the screen comes a still image of an empty, regular Sainsbury's plastic carrier bag, orange and lightweight.

"Apparently not," she says. "You'd think they'd have used something a bit sturdier, wouldn't you? I mean, those things are no good at all. One medium-sized chicken and you're lucky if you can get it from the shopping trolley into the boot of the car without the bag going."

"Is this the last item on the news?" I ask her.

"What do you mean?"

"Is this the last item? The joke item. The light relief. You think it's funny?"

"I suppose you're right," she says. "I don't imagine the owner is laughing. Where was the remote anyway?"

I leave the room and climb the stairs two at a time. I open my laptop and go online, logging on to Network Rail. I book a ticket—a single—for the morning. It's expensive, but that's too bad.

"I'm going to London tomorrow," I tell my wife later in bed.

"Are you going to look for that severed head?" she murmurs, half-asleep.

"How did you guess?" I say, but her breathing has already slowed to a regular pace.

I lie there thinking about getting up early and catching the train. I think about taking the Northern line to Highgate and finding my way on to the Parkland Walk, heading south towards Finsbury Park under the tree canopy, eventually coming across a thicket of blue and white police tape, a uniform standing guard, fielding questions, perhaps, from a female reporter. She'll be in her late twenties, working for a local paper, thinking it may not be civil war in Syria, but it's a big story nevertheless. Her big break. I'll listen in, follow her when she leaves, introduce myself. She'll be suspicious, bound to be. I'll explain that I know something,

I have information. She'll be dubious. I'll tell her I can help with identification. I just need to see a picture of the head. She must have seen one, or be able to find one. A headshot. Video removed from YouTube, grainy frame grab. She'll know all about it, she'll have access. Maybe we'll end up in a pub. Two halves of lager, one left untouched. I'll sense the possibility of the beginning of something—

It's no good. I can't sleep. I slip out of bed, reach for my dressing gown and leave the bedroom. Upstairs in my study I open the laptop. While it powers up, I turn to my right and crane my neck to look out of the window. The only reflection I see is of the bookshelves behind me. I turn back and lean forward over my desk, a middle-aged man roaming the internet in the middle of the night while his wife lies asleep, dreaming perhaps of new rooms discovered in old houses, of a more caring, less distracted husband.

I find nothing in the obvious places. A million distractions fail to distract me. I refine my search terms.

The first two links lead only to black oblongs, dead screens. Across the middle of each one runs a line: *This video does not exist*. The third link takes me to a page of text, no video. I read the report, which says nothing of interest. I go back to an earlier search term and modify it slightly. I scroll down the page of links, navigate to the second page, click on the third link down, one I have yet to try. The name of the web site is not familiar to me. In both the headline and the standfirst I am warned that the video contains "graphic images". I reflect on how the meaning of this word, "graphic", has changed over a relatively short period of time. I read a paragraph that explains the context, then scroll down and click on the arrow on the video, which starts to play. I click on the full-screen symbol.

Beneath a forget-me-not blue sky with scattered puffs of white cloud, three men kneel, heads down, on a grassy hillside, hands tied behind their backs. A man wearing an Afghan-style soft cap and carrying an automatic weapon over his shoulder addresses a crowd of men and boys who wait in patient ranks like paparazzi at a première. The man in the cap, speaking in Arabic, talks about the men kneeling on the ground, indicating them in turn. In the background another man waits, a thickset Rasputin with his long dark straggly hair and long beard and black long-skirted costume. On a sign or a word from the man in the cap, the man with the long hair and the long beard pushes the first of the three condemned men face first on to the ground. The crowd becomes excited as everyone jostles for the best positions not only to see what is happening but to film it on their cameraphones. At the same time, the crowd finds its voice. *Allahu akbar, Allahu akbar, Allahu akbar.* I turn the volume down, briefly aware of my increased heart rate. The camera on which the video is being shot momentarily cuts out and when the picture is restored the man with the long hair is straddling the first of the condemned men and sawing at his neck with a ten-inch knife. The man with the long hair keeps having to stop and start, looking for a better angle. This is no easy task. He saws and he saws at the man's neck while other necks are craning for a better view and the camera lurches to one side. A shoulder moves into shot and, by the time it is possible to see clearly once more, the job is done and another man lifts the severed head to show it to the crowd before placing it, upright, facing forwards, on the dead man's back. It no longer looks real, but nor does it resemble a prop; it exists somewhere between reality and illusion. It no longer belongs to its former owner, but is part of something else now, something more abstract. *Allahu akbar, Allahu akbar.*

Attention turns to the second of the condemned men. He is wearing a blue suit. His blindfold is removed. Immediately to his left lies the first man's corpse. The condemned man does not turn to look, but continues to stare at the ground. The man with the long hair now pushes him forwards and then on to his side. He pulls the condemned man's head back and draws the blade across his throat back and forth, back and forth, like a child with a cello. The knife is not really suitable. A man I haven't noticed before hands him another knife and he drops the first knife on the grass, which is no longer green. This is a job for a serrated knife, but these knives do not appear to be serrated and the blood will make maintaining a steady grip on the slippery handle almost impossible. But still he cuts, still he works away at the crimson gash, pulling the head back by the chin, aided by hands from the crowd that pull on the man's arm. Finally, the head is detached and the man with the long hair places it on the dead man's back just in front of his still-bound hands. Another man picks it up to show it to the crowd and then he replaces it on the dead man's back. A boy of eleven or twelve in a yellow t-shirt and blue jeans and a green sweatshirt tied around his waist approaches for a closer look. *Allahu akbar, Allahu akbar, Allahu akbar*.

The video finishes before the execution of the third man is carried out.

I click in the top left-hand corner of the window and then close the laptop. My heart is beating fast and I realise I have a headache. I stand up too quickly and have to lean on the back of the chair for support. I look around my study. Everything in it—the books, the DVDs, the magazines; my chair, the desk, my laptop—looks the same and yet different. I leave the room and stand on the upper landing gazing up at the skylight in the sloping ceiling, my arms wrapped tightly around my body. I sit down on the top step and stare into the darkness of the stairwell for an indeterminate length of time. It could be minutes; it could be an hour.

I re-enter the bedroom and walk around the end of the bed to the window. I open the curtain and stand looking out at the street in the night, focusing and unfocusing my vision. I am still standing there when it begins to get light and my reflection gradually fades. Soon I can no longer see my face, the look in my eyes.

My wife stirs. "I thought you were going to London," she says.

"No," I say. "Not any more."

Lancashire

"Nelson, Colne, Darwen," said Cassie, reading the names off the roadsigns. "I remember all these Lancashire towns from Bournemouth," she said.

"Your mam's talking nonsense again," said her husband Paul into the rear-view mirror.

"What are you talking about, Mummy?" asked James, who at ten was the elder of the two. His two front teeth still hadn't closed the gap, freckles scattered across his nose.

"From when I worked in the sorting office in Bournemouth one Christmas," Cassie explained.

"For Christmas . . . yeah . . ." began Ellie, James's younger sister, "I want an iPod Nano. A black one."

Ellie, her naturally streaked hair looking like it needed a good brush, enunciated slowly, as if she still couldn't quite believe she could speak. Or was Paul projecting his own wonder at his daughter's power of speech? She had been able to speak for years, of course, but had indeed been a slow starter.

"You can't have one," said her brother.

"Why not?"

"Because I haven't got one."

"You've got one on your Christmas list. I saw it."

"But I haven't got one yet and you can't get one at the same time as I get one. You have to wait till I've had one for six weeks. Or a year."

"No, I don't. Mummy, do I?"

"That's enough, children," said Cassie, smiling at Paul. "Look at the wonderful scenery. Isn't this lovely? Just imagine. If we'd been driving for half an hour from our old house, we wouldn't even have got beyond the North Circular."

James and Ellie ignored this, bent over PSP and Gameboy respectively, articulating their thumbs in ways their parents had never learned to do. Paul wondered how long it would be before Ellie decided she also had to graduate from a Gameboy to a PSP.

Sunlight flashed across the windscreen, sparkling in a scattering of raindrops and temporarily blinding him.

"Are you keeping your eye on the map?" he asked Cassie.

"Just keep going on the A666," said Cassie. "All the way."

"Right through Blackburn?" he asked, blinking.

"Right on past these dark Satanic mills," she said as they passed another refurbished chimney.

"Mummy?"

"Do you know what I read the other day?" said Paul. "I read that 'dark Satanic mills' was never meant to imply this sort of thing—" he waved his hand at yet another converted mill—"the industrial revolution and all that. What Blake was really talking about, apparently, were Oxford and Cambridge universities."

"Mummy?"

"What, darling?"

"What does Satanic mean?"

"Oh, really, Paul?" said Paul, pretending to mimic Cassie. "That's fascinating, Paul. Thank you for sharing that, Paul."

"Ask your dad, Ellie. He seems to know all about it." Cassie placed her hand on Paul's leg and smiled at him. "It was fascinating, darling. I didn't know that, actually."

"It's only conjecture. Academic gossip, you know."

"Are we nearly there?" asked James.

"That's a good question," said Cassie, looking at Paul. "*Are* we nearly there?"

"You tell me. You've got the map." Paul's lips straightened into a suppressed smile.

Conversation was soon restricted to the essentials of navigation while they negotiated Blackburn.

"Who are we going to see again?" James asked as they found their way back on to the A666.

"Penny and Howard. Friends of your mam's."

"Howard and Penny, friends of your dad's more like," said Cassie.

"I thought we were going to see Connor," said James.

"We are," said Paul. "Connor is Penny and Howard's son."

"Are those the people we met in the park?" James asked.

"You know they are. Now, shush, matey. I've got to read the signs."

"Your dad needs all his concentration to read the signs. A lot of men find it very, very hard reading signs."

Paul smiled, then frowned at a hidden sign.

"What did that say? Did that say Wilpshire?"

They turned off the A666 and within a couple of minutes pulled up outside a well-kept Victorian semi. Pampas grasses grew in the lawned garden, steps led up to the front door. Paul pulled on the handbrake.

"Paul, I hope this is going to be all right," Cassie said quietly. "I mean, we barely know these people."

"It's a little late for that," Paul answered.

"We've been out with them, what, twice for drinks?"

"You know what they say about pampas grasses, don't you?" Paul muttered.

"What?" came James's voice from the back.

"Never you mind," said Paul. "It'll be fine. Penny's into stained glass, remember. If you run out of things to talk about, just talk about stained glass. Did you know, children, that your mam's in the *Guinness Book of Records* for length of time talking about stained glass?"

"What about you and Howard?" asked Cassie with an indulgent smile.

"We'll have something in common. Didn't he say he liked punk and new wave? Late '70s, '80s music? In any case, no one expects blokes to talk. We just have to sit there looking like we're not having a shit time. Anyway," he added, "this is for the children, isn't it? They liked Connor when they met him in the park. And it's kind of them to invite us. Perhaps they know what it's like to be new to an area."

Cassie was the first to become aware of the front door opening and Penny and Howard appeared, all smiles. The child, Connor, squeezed between their legs and ran down the path towards them.

"Here goes," she said as she opened the car door.

They got the standard tour.

Downstairs rooms tastefully restored, with an attractive archway ("Looks original. I don't know, maybe 1920s") connecting them. Kitchen long and narrow—"We're going to open it up at the back—here and here—and have lovely big French windows where that corner is," said Penny. "It's lovely how it is," flattered Cassie. "What, all this clinker? Tongue and groove? Ugh." And so it went on. Upstairs, Connor's bedroom ("Is this really my room?" Strange child. Though weren't all children strange, apart from your own, Cassie thought), amazingly tidy for a ten-year-old's; Penny and Howard's room, drawers and wardrobes neatly closed; and a tiny office for Penny ("Oh, you know, PR," she said with a modest, almost dismissive wave of the hand, when asked to remind them what she did)—a filing cabinet, a laptop closed on a little table, a suspiciously tidy desk-tidy, a pile of magazines (*Lancashire*

Life, *Closer*, *OK*). And finally the converted attic, double bed, fresh towels. Velux windows—"You can see Blackpool Tower on a good day."

It wasn't a good day.

Back downstairs a bottle of Pinot Grigio was opened for Cassie and Penny, and local beers broken out for the boys.

"Boys," said Penny with a little laugh.

The children had stayed upstairs with Connor.

"Is this Wire?" Paul asked, glancing at the stereo. "Early Wire, by the sound of it."

"Yes, it's *Pink Flag*," said Howard.

"Oh, they're off," said Penny, leaning towards Cassie on the leather sofa and dropping her hand briefly on her knee.

Flashes of red and green lit up the sky outside the window, followed by a bang.

"It's not fireworks night yet, is it?" asked Paul.

"We've not had Halloween yet," Cassie said.

"I remember when fireworks were saved until Guy Fawkes' Night, and Halloween was neither here nor there," said Howard.

"Mmm," agreed Paul. "Nice beer," he added, holding his glass up to the halogen lighting to admire its golden-brown colour.

Howard passed him the bottle.

"Pendle Witches' Brew," Paul read from the label.

"Pendle Hill's just up the road," Howard offered.

"It's very good of you to invite us over," Paul heard Cassie saying to Penny.

"We know what it's like when you've just moved somewhere new," Penny said in response.

"It was weird that day in the park," Cassie said. "You and I met pretty much exactly at the same time as Howard and Paul bumped into each other right over the other side of the park."

"I remember you had Ellie with you in the playground," said Penny, "and I assumed it was just the two of you. Then you told me your husband and son were somewhere kicking a football. And a minute later they turned up—with Howard and Connor."

"What were you doing there anyway," Cassie asked, "so far from home?"

There was a moment's silence. Paul looked up and saw Penny staring into her wine glass.

"We'd been for a walk, hadn't we, darling? In Fletcher Moss Gardens," said Howard.

"Yes, of course," said Penny, getting to her feet. "I'm just going to check on the hotpot."

"Lancashire hotpot!" exclaimed Paul in delight.

"Is there any other kind?"

"So, have you not been here long?" Cassie asked Howard.

"Oh dear, is it that obvious?" Howard said, and Paul saw Cassie colour up. "No, we haven't been here that long, hence the drive down to south Manchester to investigate Fletcher Moss. We're still seeing the sights."

"I think I'll go and see if Penny wants a hand," said Cassie, and Paul raised his glass to his lips to hide his look of dismay.

"Lovely house," he said, his eyes scanning the walls. There was a handful of pictures, but they were beyond bland, the sort of thing you might buy for a fiver in IKEA. "Do you mind?" he asked as he got up and walked over to check out the CD collection.

"Go ahead. A lot of stuff's still in storage. That's just what I couldn't bear to be parted from."

Joy Division, The Cure, Buzzcocks, UK Subs.

"What's your favourite Cure album?" he asked Howard.

"Oh, I don't know. Remind me which ones are up there."

"*Seventeen Seconds, Pornography, Faith, Disintegration . . .* "

"Er, I really don't know. *Disintegration*, perhaps."

"Mm-hmm. 'The Hanging Garden' is an amazing track, isn't it?"

"Fantastic."

Paul moved away from the CD collection and noticed an Ordnance Survey map folded up on the mantelpiece.

"I love OS maps," he said. "May I?"

"Of course."

Paul spread the map out on the coffee table. The conurbations of Blackburn, Accrington and Burnley looked like clots in the green lungs of Lancashire.

"Can you see Barnoldswick?" Howard asked, kneeling down next to Paul. "See how big it is considering it's not even on an A-road? That's because of the Rolls-Royce factory."

"Oh, right."

"All these little villages here—" Howard pointed to the section of the map between Burnley and the moors above Hebden Bridge—"the roads just run into the hills and stop. Interesting places. Lots of unusual traditions and rituals . . . "

"Really?" Paul was interested, but they heard Penny calling everyone from the kitchen.

The children came running downstairs. Paul caught James and gave him a bear hug. As the boy struggled to get free, Paul ruffled his hair.

"Good kids," Howard said.

"Yeah, we're lucky. They leapt at the chance to come here so they could see Connor again."

Howard's lips stretched over his teeth in an approximation of a smile.

In the converted attic, Paul and Cassie lay side by side. Cassie was reading a Jackie Kay collection; in an effort to meet some new people, she had joined a book club. Paul was making inroads into a thriller by Stephen Gallagher but was finding it hard to concentrate.

"Cassie?"

"Hmm?" Not looking up.

"Don't you think they're a bit odd? Howard and Penny. Don't you think there's something about them that's not quite right?"

"Hmm?"

"I'm serious."

Finally, Cassie looked up. She closed her book but kept her place with a thumb.

"You've had too much to drink."

"I only had two beers."

"That second one was quite strong."

"Do you know what it was called? It was called Nightmare. Can you believe it?"

"Another local brew?" There was a faintly patronising tone in Cassie's voice, as if she regarded the interest in local beers as endearing, a "boy" thing.

"It's actually from Yorkshire, but Yorkshire's just up the road. Something to do with the Legend of the White Horse."

"I hope it doesn't *give* you nightmares."

"I felt at times tonight as if I might be having one, actually."

"Was the hotpot a bit too fatty for you?"

"That was all right. It was the warm salad with black pudding I wasn't sure about."

"Faddy. I think Penny and Howard are very nice and they've been very kind."

"There's just something about them. It's hard to put my finger on. Howard thought 'The Hanging Garden' by The Cure was on *Disintegration*, but it's not. It's on *Pornography*."

"Big deal." A little impatience was starting to creep into Cassie's voice.

"But these were CDs he said he couldn't bear to be parted from. I just got the impression they were trying a bit too hard to get us to like them. Or trust them."

"Don't be silly. We just have some shared interests. Like stained glass."

Paul laughed. "I thought you and Penny were never going to shut up about stained glass at the dinner table."

"Common interests, that's all it is. Now do you think we could get some sleep? They said they'd show us a bit of the countryside in the morning."

But sleep was a long time coming, for Paul at least.

Paul wanted his dream to continue. In fact, he was convinced it would continue with or without him. The question was whether he could remain part of it. His journey towards full consciousness became a struggle between his strong attachment to the dream—the grammar and meaning of which were losing coherence by the second—and his acknowledgement of responsibility. The day, he sensed, was bringing anxiety, though from what quarter he did not know. Within a few more seconds the warp of reality had completely overpowered the weft of the dream and Paul felt a sudden, inexplicable panic. He sat up and hurriedly pulled on his clothes. Cassie woke and asked him what the matter was, but he couldn't bring himself to answer.

Seconds later he was taking the stairs two at a time down to the next floor, where the children had slept in Connor's bedroom. He opened the door. The room was as quiet as the rest of the house. The curtains were still drawn and the room was dark, but he saw instantly that not only was the bed empty, but the two sleeping bags were as well, left untidily where they lay like the discarded casings of chrysalises.

Paul backed out on to the landing and descended swiftly to the ground floor. Marching down the hall as if wading through treacle, he glanced into the living room, which looked no livelier than the bedroom, and approached the closed door that led to the kitchen. He watched as his hand reached out to open it and the next thing he saw was Penny standing at the sink and beyond her were James and Ellie sat at the table eating croissants and *pains au chocolat* with Connor. All three had chocolate rings around their mouths.

Paul felt confused and relieved at the same time. He said hello and accepted Penny's offer of a pot of tea and retreated, saying he would be back down in a minute. As he passed the living room he saw Howard bent over the coffee table studying the map.

"Morning," said Howard.

"Hi."

As Paul climbed the stairs, he tried to calm himself down, as there was clearly no sense in sharing any of this with Cassie. She met him on the first-floor landing and they went back down to the kitchen together.

Once breakfast was over and the children were dressed, everyone moved towards the front door. Paul and Cassie stepped onto the garden path. Paul took the bags to the car, while Cassie waited for the children. He packed the boot and leaned against the car, enjoying the view over the fields and feeling sheepish for his strange behaviour and yet pretty good about everything, considering. He took in a deep breath and let it out slowly, enjoying the purely physical sensation of filling and emptying his lungs. Over there were Blackburn, Accrington and Burnley, yet he could see nothing but green.

Cassie joined him and told him that the children wanted to go in Connor's car.

"Fine," he said and opened the driver's door to get in.

"Their car's around the back," Cassie said.

"No problem. We wait here, yeah?"

Cassie nodded and Paul looked in the rear-view mirror. It didn't matter how much the children might occasionally bicker in the back of the car, when they weren't there he missed them.

Two or three minutes went by and Howard and Penny still hadn't shown up. Paul kept checking the rear-view mirror.

"How long does it take to strap three kids into a car?" he asked.

Cassie shook her head.

"Maybe they're arguing over who sits where?" she said. "You know what they're like."

"Not usually when it's someone else's car," said Paul. "I daresay Howard's a safe driver," he added after a moment.

Cassie, who would know what was going through Paul's mind, said, "How do *you* drive when you have someone else's child in the back? Recklessly or even more safely than usual?"

"Yeah, you're right. As usual," he said, with a little smile. "But what's taking them so long?"

They waited a further minute then Paul got out of the car and wandered down to the lane that led to the back of the house. There was no sign of a vehicle making its way down towards him, so he had a quick look back at Cassie sitting in their car and started walking up the lane. He reached a track on the left, which could only be the access to the rear of Howard and Penny's house. Still no sign of their car. He ran down the little track towards the back of their house, which he isolated from its neighbours. There was no car. He looked around wildly, suddenly feeling exactly as he had done upon waking when he had been convinced, for whatever reason, that the children were no longer in the house.

At his feet in the mud was a set of tyre tracks. They led towards the lane and then turned left rather than right.

There had to be another way around to the front of the house. He turned right and ran back to the road, where Cassie was still sitting waiting in the car.

"Have you seen them?" he asked breathlessly as he reached the car.

"What do you mean?"

"The car's gone. They've gone. They've all gone. They've got the children!"

"Maybe they're coming another way round?"

"They're not. They'd have been here by now. They've gone and they've taken the children. I don't know why, but they've taken the children. Oh Jesus Christ!"

They looked at each other and for a moment said nothing. Paul's breath froze in the air in little clouds.

"Call the police," said Cassie. "No, wait. Maybe they're still in the house? They got delayed or they're playing a joke."

"There's no car at the back."

"Let's check the house."

Together they ran up the front path. The door was locked so Paul knocked hard. When no one came he put his elbow through the stained glass and reached inside to open the door. They entered the house. Paul ran upstairs. Cassie went to check the living room and the kitchen. He could hear her, for some reason, opening and closing cupboard doors.

"Paul!" she shouted upstairs.

"Cassie!" he shouted down from above. "Come up here!" She ran upstairs.

"All the downstairs cupboards are empty," she said.

"Look!" he said.

The filing cabinet in Penny's office was empty. The laptop had disappeared from the table. The desk-tidy was as suspiciously tidy as before. In the bedroom that they had said was theirs, the wardrobes contained nothing but a few rattling wire hangers. In Connor's room it was the same story. Drawers filled with stale air. Empty cupboards that they had presumed were stuffed with toys.

No one lived in this house. No one at all.

Acknowledgments

The author wishes to thank the editors and publishers
of those magazines and anthologies in which some
of these stories first appeared. The author would also like
to thank Brian J. Showers of The Swan River Press.

"The Other Man"
was first published in *Black Wings II*,
edited by S.T. Joshi, PS Publishing, 2012.

"The Blind Man"
was first published in *Still*,
edited by Roelof Bakker,
Negative Press London, 2012.

"Sitting Tenant"
was first published in *Poe's Progeny*,
edited by Gary Fry, Gray Friar Press, 2005.

"The Trees"
was first published in *Dark Voices 6*,
edited by David Sutton and Stephen Jones,
Pan Books, 1994.

Acknowledgments

"Hide and Seek"
was first published in *Dark Terrors 6*,
edited by Stephen Jones and David Sutton,
Victor Gollancz, 2002.

"The Dummy"
was first published in *The New Uncanny*,
edited by Sarah Eyre and Ra Page,
Comma Press, 2008.

"Maths Tower"
was first published in *The Flash*,
edited by Peter Wild, Social Disease, 2007.

"Dead End"
was first published in *X7*,
edited by Alex Davis, KnightWatch Press, 2013.

"The Cellar"
was first published in *Four For Fear*,
edited by Peter Crowther,
PS Publishing, 2012.

"The Reunion"
was first published in *Poe*,
edited by Ellen Datlow, Solaris, 2009.

"Moving Out"
was first published in *Skeleton Crew*,
edited by Dave Reeder, January 1991.

"Jayne Anne Phillips"
was first published in *The London Magazine*,
edited by Sara-Mae Tuson, February/March 2008.

"The Family Room"
was first published in *Taverns of the Dead*,
edited by Kealan Patrick Burke,
Cemetery Dance Publications, 2005.

"Cuckoo"
was first published in *Riptide* Issue 5,
edited by Jane Feaver, Dirt Pie Press, 2010.

"This Video Does Not Exist"
was first published in *The Spectral Book of Horror Stories*,
edited by Mark Morris, Spectral Press, 2014.

"Lancashire"
was first published in *Phobic: Modern Horror Stories*,
edited by Andy Murray, Comma Press, 2007.

"The Blink" and "The Empty Flat"
appear for the first time in this collection.

About the Author

Nicholas Royle is the author of four other short story collections—*Mortality*, *Ornithology*, *London Gothic*, and *Manchester Uncanny*—and seven novels, including *Counterparts*, *Antwerp*, and *First Novel*. He has edited more than twenty-five anthologies and is series editor of *Best British Short Stories*. He runs Nightjar Press, which publishes original short stories as signed, numbered chapbooks. His English translation of Vincent de Swarte's 1998 novel *Pharricide* was published by Confingo Publishing in 2019. In 2021 his first book of non-fiction, *White Spines: Confessions of a Book Collector*, was published by Salt.

SWAN RIVER PRESS

Founded in 2003, Swan River Press is an independent publishing company, based in Dublin, Ireland, dedicated to gothic, supernatural, and fantastic literature. We specialise in limited edition hardbacks, publishing fiction from around the world with an emphasis on Ireland's contributions to the genre.

www.swanriverpress.ie

"Handsome, beautifully made volumes . . . altogether irresistible."

– Michael Dirda, *Washington Post*

"It [is] often down to small, independent, specialist presses to keep the candle of horror fiction flickering . . . "

– Darryl Jones, *Irish Times*

"Swan River Press has emerged as one of the most inspiring new presses over the past decade. Not only are the books beautifully presented and professionally produced, but they aspire consistently to high literary quality and originality, ranging from current writers of supernatural/weird fiction to rare or forgotten works by departed authors."

– Peter Bell, *Ghosts & Scholars*

THE ANNIVERSARY
OF NEVER

Joel Lane

Joel Lane's award-winning stories have been widely praised, notably by other masters of weird fiction such as M. John Harrison, Graham Joyce, and Ramsey Campbell. His tales also regularly appeared in the "best of" annual anthologies of Ellen Datlow, Karl Edward Wagner, and Stephen Jones. With this posthumous collection, Lane continues his unflinching exploration of the human condition. "*The Anniversary of Never* is a group of tales concerned with the theme of the afterlife," observed Lane, "and the idea that we may enter the afterlife before death, or find parts of it in our world." These stories of love and death will burrow deep into the reader's mind and impregnate it with a vision often as bleak as the night is black.

"Melancholy and bleak, the weird, often dark stories
in this slim, beautiful volume are a fitting coda
to Lane's life and work."

– Ellen Datlow

"A liminal collection whose ghost like state almost mimics
that of much of the material contained within its pages."

– Black Static

"Rich and varied forms of darkness
illuminated by the author's wit and intelligence."

– Supernatural Tales

YOU'LL KNOW WHEN YOU GET THERE

Lynda E. Rucker

A woman returns home to revisit an encounter with the numinous; couples take up residence in houses full of sinister secrets; a man fleeing a failed marriage discovers something ancient and unknowable in rural Ireland . . .

In her introduction, Lisa Tuttle observes that "certain places are doomed, dangerous in some inexplicable, metaphysical way", and the characters in these stories all seem drawn in their own ways to just such places, whether trying to return home or endeavouring to get as far from life as possible. These nine stories by Shirley Jackson Award winner Lynda E. Rucker tell tales of those lost and searching, often for something they cannot name, and encountering along the way the uncanny embedded in the everyday world.

"Indirection is a special skill and it's one that Lynda E. Rucker uses frequently to emphasise those near indefinable moments of social alienation and paranoia, that you just want to get up and run far, far away from."

– Adam L. G. Nevill

"Lynda is the genuine article—a serious, literary author of 'quiet horror' whose work is disquieting, inspiring, and oddly reassuring. It's good to know that there are writers so gifted working in our genre."

– *Supernatural Tales*

THE DARK RETURN OF TIME

R. B. Russell

"I was searching for The Dark Return of Time on the 'net. It's odd, but there isn't a copy for sale anywhere, and it doesn't turn up on the British Library catalogue, the Library of Congress website, or the Biblioteque Nationale."

The past doesn't always stay where it should. It is as though somebody, or something, is forever trying to bring it painfully into the present.

Flavian Bennett is trying to leave his past behind when he goes to work in his father's bookshop in Paris. But a curious customer, Reginald Hopper, is desperate to resurrect his own murky origins. Hopper believes that a rare and mysterious book, The Dark Return of Time, may be the key to what happened before he arrived in Paris. In this quiet thriller by R. B. Russell, the futures—and pasts—of these two men will soon cross.

"A beautifully written and very clever work of art."

– Black Static

"R. B. Russell's The Dark Return of Time . . . *is a short thriller that opens in a shop selling second-hand books in Paris. What could be better?"*

– Michael Dirda, *Washington Post*